44

Fans of tha... ...Pohl and C. M.
Kornbluth ... ...ction of nine of
their justly ... ...es are top-flight
and varied ... ...otely resembles
another. Here are tales of time travel, the Third (or Fourth?)
World War, civilizations aeons in the future, weird and
wonderful technology and commonplace things with an
uncommon slant. Each will take the reader – fan and newcomer
alike – far into the fertile imaginary worlds and times of the
most famous SF writing duo ever.

'The cream of the 35 they jointly wrote. They're well worth
preserving'
Manchester Evening News

'They are clever stories, and reality is not entirely banished;
one immediately likes any collection that contains such a jolter
as ['The World of Myrion Flowers']'
Brian Aldiss – Oxford Mail

Also by Frederik Pohl in Panther Books

The Frederik Pohl Omnibus

Frederik Pohl
and
C. M. Kornbluth

The Wonder Effect

Panther

Granada Publishing Limited
Published in 1974 by Panther Books Ltd
Frogmore, St Albans, Herts AL2 2NF

First published in Great Britain by Victor Gollancz Ltd 1967
Copyright © Frederik Pohl 1962
Best Friend – Copyright © Fictioneers, Inc 1941
Critical Mass – Copyright © Galaxy Publishing Corporation 1961
The Engineer – Copyright © Royal Publications, Inc 1955
A Gentle Dying – Copyright © Galaxy Publishing Corporation 1961
Mars-Tube – Copyright © Fictioneers, Inc 1941
Nightmare with Zeppelins – Copyright © Galaxy Publishing Corporation 1958
The Quaker Cannon – Copyright © Street and Smith Publications, Inc 1961
Trouble in Time – Copyright Fictioneers, Inc 1940
The World of Myrion Flowers – Copyright © Mercury Press, Inc 1961
Made and printed in Great Britain by
Richard Clay (The Chaucer Press) Ltd
Bungay, Suffolk
Set in Linotype Plantin

Contents

Introduction

Cyril Kornbluth, who was my good friend as well as my collaborator over a period of two decades, was seventeen years old when we first began writing stories together. I was not quite twenty. Neither of us was entirely an amateur – I was editing two science-fiction magazines, long since perished, and Cyril had already published three or four science-fiction stories – but we were so near to it as made no difference, and many of our writing habits were formed at the same time, writing the same stories.

In all, we wrote together seven published novels and perhaps thirty-five short stories. The short stories were what we did first, and most of them are awful. Of the thirty or so of these which we wrote from 1939 to 1943 at least twenty-five will forever remain buried under the pseudonyms under which they were first published, if I have anything to say about it; but a few of them do seem to be worth another look, and they are included in this collection.

Then we both went into the Army in World War II. The idea of writing anything, particularly science fiction, seemed pretty remote to both of us. I recently came across a letter Cyril wrote to me while he was a machine-gunner in Belgium and I was a weatherman near Foggia in which he said, 'I'm afraid science fiction has had it, killed by radar and the sniperscope.' I don't remember whether I agreed or not. Certainly it seemed like a logical point of view at the time. Science had caught up with science fiction and there didn't seem to be much future for the art ... Less than a year later we were both civilians and both writing science fiction again; but Cyril was in Chicago, a newsman employed by a wire service, and I was writing advertising copy for an agency in New York, and we didn't collaborate again until 1951, when we wrote *The Space Merchants*.

A number of reviewers have speculated, and readers from time to time ask, what the mechanics of collaboration were between us. I take this to condone the vanity of supplying an answer. There isn't one single answer, though, because we tried everything. At first I made up plots, Cyril fleshed out the stories and I rewrote them in final form for publication. That was the technique that produced the bulk of the early stories which I now hope to see forgotten. It was not a very good way of writing a story, and we never wrote a complete story that way after 1942. (I do retain some fondness for a few stories produced under that scheme. *Best Friend, Mars-Tube* and *Trouble in Time* were written that way.)

The Space Merchants was written on an entirely different basis. I had written the first twenty thousand words of this story with the intention of doing it all by myself; but I showed it to Horace Gold, editing *Galaxy Magazine*, who wanted to publish it as a serial – not in ten years or when I got around to finishing it, but soon. Cyril had just come East. I showed him the part I had written and asked if he wanted to come in on it; he did; he went home and wrote the next twenty thousand words or so and then, turn and turn about, we wrote the last third of the book together.

That turned out to be a remarkably pleasant way to write a book. As we ultimately refined the process, we would spend a day or two talking out ideas and plot and then go on a concentrated, around-the-clock schedule, one working while the other slept, of producing manuscript in five-page chunks. What emerged was a good, healthy first draft. There were always revisions, which I usually did; but the changes were mostly cosmetic. The watch-on watch-off writing was generally done at my house in New Jersey, where Cyril had a room permanently set aside for him, and thus, in alternate increments of 1,500 words or so, we constructed *Search the Sky, Gladiator-at-Law* and most of our three novels which were outside the science-fiction field. (Two of these were done wholly in this way. The third was like *The Space Merchants* in reverse;

Cyril had begun a novel and was behind schedule and we finished it together.)

I don't know how well this system would work for anyone else. We had the advantage of long practice – and of having done some of our growing up together, so that our attitudes were more or less similar. Quite often a species of telepathy seemed to come into it. Several times I ended a page in the middle of a sentence and discovered, when it came my turn again, that Cyril had used the exact wording I had had in mind to complete it.

Wolfbane was a different sort of story. We planned it as a 15,000 word novelette—and wrote it that way, too, turn and about. But it was almost unreadable, far too telegraphic and compressed; and I opened it out to about 40,000 words, in which form it was published as a magazine serial; whereafter Cyril expanded it to about 60,000 words for the final book version. This was almost the last writing Cyril did before his death.

Of the stories in this volume, *The Engineer* was the only short we wrote together in the period between *The Space Merchants* and *Wolfbane*, and it was an accident. (In a different form, it was intended to have been a sequence in one of the novels.) *A Gentle Dying*, which was one of the last of our stories to be published, was actually almost the first we wrote. The manuscript was misplaced for years and did not turn up again until Cyril had died. The remaining stories in this book are all projects which were incomplete at his death, and which I subsequently completed. There are still one or two lost manuscripts, but it isn't very likely that they will turn up at this date, and barring such event there will be no more.

As this is not an obituary for Cyril Kornbluth but only a note on some of the stories we wrote together, I do not suppose it fitting to dwell on personal matters. But Cyril was a good man: intelligent, able, illuminating every gathering in which he took part. It was a pleasure to work with him. I cannot say how much I regret that it is over.   *Frederik Pohl*

Critical Mass

I

The neutron was a plump young man named Walter Chase, though what he thought he was was a brand-new Engineering graduate, sitting mummified and content with the other 3,876 in Eastern's class of '98, waiting for his sheepskin.

The university glee club sang the ancient scholastic song *Gaudeamus Igitur* with mournful respect and creamy phrasing, for they and most of the graduates, faculty members, parents, relatives and friends present in the field house thought it was a hymn instead of the rowdy drinking song it was. It was a warm June day, conducive to reverence. Of Eastern's 3,877 graduating men and women only three had majored in classical languages. What those three would do for a living from July on was problematical. But in June they had at least the pleasure of an internal chuckle over the many bowed heads.

Walter Chase's was bowed with the rest. He was of the Civil Engineering breed, and he had learned more about concrete in the four years just ended than you would think possible. Something called The Cement Research and Development Institute, whose vague but inspirational commercials were regularly on the TV screens, had located Walter as a promising high-school graduate. He was then considering the glamorous and expensive field of nuclear physics. A plausible C.R.D.I. field man had signed him up and set him straight. It took twelve years to make a nuclear physicist. Now, wasn't that a hell of a long time to wait for the good things of life? Now, here was something he ought to consider: Four years. In four years he could walk right into a job with automatic pay raises, protected seniority, stock participation *and* Blue Everything, paid by the company. Concrete was the big industry of tomorrow. The C.R.D.I. was deeply concerned over the lack of interest in concrete engineering, and it was prepared to do something about it: full four-year scholarship, tuition, living costs and pocket money. Well?

Walter signed. He was a level-headed eighteen-year-old. He had been living with a pinch-penny aunt and uncle, his parents dead; the chance of the aunt and uncle financing twelve years of nuclear studies for him he estimated to lie midway between the incredible and the impossible.

Two solid hours dwindled past in addresses by the Chancellor, the Governor of the State and a couple of other politicos receiving honorary degrees. Walter Chase allowed the words to slip past him as though they were dreams, although many of them concerned his own speciality: shelters. You knew what politician talk was. He and the 3,876 others were coldly realistic enough to know that C.S.B. was a long way from being enacted into law, much less concrete-and-steel Civilian Shelters in fact. Otherwise why would the Institute have to keep begging for students to give scholarships to? He drowsed. Then, as if with an absent-minded start, the program ended.

Everybody flocked away on to the campus.

In the hubbub was all the talk of the time: 'Nice weather, but, Kee-*rist*! those speeches!' 'Who d'ya like in the All-Star?' 'Nothing wrong with C.S.B. if it's *handled* right, but you take and throw a couple thousand warheads over the Pole and —' 'My feet hurt.' Chase heard without listening. He was in a hurry.

There was no one he wanted to meet, no special friend or family. The aunt and uncle were not present at his graduation. When it had become clear from their letters that they expected him to pay back what they had spent to care for him as soon as he began earning money, he telephoned them. Collect. He suggested that they sue him for the money or, alternatively, take a flying jump for themselves. It effectively closed out a relationship he loathed.

Chase saw, approaching him across the crowded campus, another relationship it was time to close out. The relationship's name was Douglasina MacArthur Baggett, a brand-new grad-

uate in journalism. She was pretty and she had in tow two
older persons who Chase perceived to be the parents. 'Walter,'
she bubbled. 'I don't believe you were even *looking* for me!
Meet Daddy and Mom.'

Walter Chase allowed his hand to be shaken. Baggett *père*
was something in Health, Education and Welfare that had
awakened Walter's interest at one time; but as Douglasina had
let it slip that Daddy had been passed over for promotion three
years running, Walter's interest had run out. The old fool now
began babbling about how young fellows like Walter would,
through the Civilian Shelters Bill, really give the country the
top-dog Summit bargaining position that would pull old
Zhdetchnikov's cork for him. The mother simpered: 'So
you're the young man! We've heard so much about you in
Douglasina's letters. I tell you, why don't you come and spend
the All-Star weekend with us in Chevy Chase?'

Walter asked blankly: 'Why?'

'Why?' said Mrs. Baggett in a faint voice, after a perceptible pause. Walter smiled warmly.

'After all,' he said, shrugging, 'boy–girl college friendships.
... She's a fine girl, Mrs. Baggett. Delighted to have met you,
Mr. Baggett. Doug, maybe we'll run into each other again,
eh?' He clapped her on the shoulder and slipped away.

Once screened from the sight of their faces, he sighed. In
some ways he would miss her, he thought. Well. On to the
future!

In the dormitory he snapped the locks on his luggage, already
packed, carried them down to be stowed in the luggage compartment of the airport bus and then circulated gently through
the halls. He had in four years at Eastern made eleven Good
Contacts and thirty-six Possibles, and he had an hour or two
before his plane to joke with, shake the hand of, or congratulate the nine of those on the list who shared his dorm. He
fooled the fools and flatered the flatterable, but in his wake a
few of his classmates grimly said: 'That young son of a bitch

is going to go far, unless he runs out of faces to step on.'

Having attended to his nine he charitably spread some of his remaining time among the couple dozen Outside Chances he ran into. To a sincere, but confused, servo-mech specialist he said, man-to-man, 'Well, Frankie, what's the big decision? Made up your mind about the job yet?'

The servo-mech man clutched him and told him his tale of woe. 'God no, Walt. I don't know *which* way to turn. Missile R & D's offering me a commission right away, captain inside of two years. But who wants to be a soldier all his life? And there's nothing in private industry for inertial guidance, you know. Damn it, Walt, if only they let you resign from the service after a couple years!' Chase said something more or less comforting and moved on. He was careful not to chuckle until he was out of sight.

Poor Frankie! Got himself educated in what amounted to a military speciality – who else could afford servo-mechanisms? – and discovered he hated the Army.

Still, Chase meditated while nodding, smiling and hand-shaking, thirty years as an Engineering Officer might not be so bad. As it was one of the alternatives open to himself – that was what C.S.B. was all about – he allowed his mind to drift over the prospects. It wasn't like the bad old days of fighting. A flat and rigid policy of atomic retaliation had been U. S. military doctrine for fifty-three years, and backing it up was a large, well-trained U. S. military establishment of career men. And the regulations said *career*. The only way out short of thirty-year retirement was with a can tied to your tail and a taint to your name. He dismissed that thirty-year dead end with light contempt, as he had before.

The air-raid warning sirens began to howl their undulating hysteria.

Chase sighed and glanced at his watch. Not too bad. He should still be able to make his plane. Everyone around him was saying things like, 'Ah, damn it!' or 'Oh, dear,' or '*Jeez*!' But they were all dutifully following the arrows and the 'S' signs that dotted the campus.

Chase trailed along. He was kind of annoyed, but nothing could really spoil his day. The first shelter he came to was full up. The freshman raid warden stood at the door – Chase had been a raid warden himself three years before – chanting: 'Basement filled to capacity, folks. Please proceed to Chemistry building. Don't block the exit, folks. Basement here filled —'

Because of the extra crowd caused by the graduation the Chemistry building basement was filled, too, but Chase got into the Administration building and sat down to wait. Like everybody else. Women fussed about their dresses – they always had, in every air raid drill he had taken part in, say, four a week for fifty-two weeks of each year for the nearly twenty years since he had been old enough to toddle alongside his late mother and father. Men grumbled about missing appointments. *They* always had. But for the most part the battery-fed air-raid lights gleamed equally on them all, the warden fussed with the air conditioner and the younger folk smooched in the corners.

It wasn't a bad shelter, Walter Chase thought. The Law School basement was a mess – too high a pH in the mortar mix, and the aggregate showing hygroscopic tendencies because of some clown not watching his rock crusher, so the walls were cracked and damp. Chemistry's had been poured in a freeze. Well, naturally it began to sinter and flake. This was better; trust the Chancellor to make sure his own nest was downy! Of course, in a *raid* none of them would be worth a hoot; but there weren't to be any real raids. Ever.

A jet plane's ripping path sounded overhead.

Evidently this was going to be a full-dress affair, at least regional in scope. They didn't throw simulated manned-bomber attacks for a purely local do. Walter frowned. It had suddenly occurred to him that with the air-transport flight lanes screwed up by military fighters on simulated missions everything within a thousand miles might be rerouted into stack patterns. What the devil would that do to his plane's departure time?

Then he smiled forebearingly. He was, in a way, pleased to be annoyed. It meant he was entering into the adult world of appointments and passages. They said that when a raid drill began to be a damn interruption instead of a welcome break from classes and a chance to smooch, then, brother, you were growing up. He guessed he was growing up.

'Goddam foolishness,' growled the man who sat next to Chase on the bench, as though it were a personal attack. More jets shredded sound overhead and he glared at Chase. Walter inventoried his English shoes, seal ring and pale cigar and at once engaged him in conversation. The man was some graduate's father; they had got separated in the raid drill, and Pop was sore as a tramped bunion. The whole drill thing was damned childishness, didn't Walter see that? And *vindictive* damned childishness when they chose to throw one on graduation day of a major university. If only Crockhouse had been elected in '96 instead of Braden, with his packed ballots in Indiana and Puerto Rico!

Here Walter Chase's interest cooled, because Pop sounded like a politician, revealed himself to be a Nationalist and thus was out of power. But there was no escaping the bench. What Pop objected bitterly to was the multiple levels of expense. Here the drill was knocking men out of production, but the damn Middle-Road Congress said they had to be paid anyhow. And if the Defense Department was making it a full-scale simulated raid, did Walter know what that meant? That meant that there went thirty or forty *Nineveh Ables* at a hundred and fifty thousand dollars apiece, and was that enough? No. Then they sent up four or five *Tyres* at ninety thousand apiece to knock down the *Ninevehs*. Did that make sense? He paused to glare at Walter Chase.

Walter said, 'Well, that's the Cold War for you. Say, who

d'you like in the All-Star —' He didn't get to finish the sentence.

'L.A.' snapped Pop, without losing a beat. 'Get the damn monkey-business over with, that's what I say. I'm a sneak-puncher and I'm proud of it. If we'd put our man in the White House instead of that psalm-singing Braden there wouldn't *be* any Moscow or Peking or Calcutta by now and we wouldn't be sitting here on our butts!'

Somebody clawed through from the bench in front; with horror, Chase recognized old man Bagget. But Douglasina's Daddy did not recognize him. Flushed with rage and politics he had eyes only for the sneak-punch advocate. 'You're right it's monkey-business, fatmouth!' he snarled. 'No thanks to you and your Crockhouse we aren't dead in this cellar instead of safe and secure! President Braden is a hundred per cent pledged to the C.S.B., God bless it, and —'

The rest of his sentence and Sneak-Punch's angry reply were drowned out by a further flight of jets overhead, and then the *wham-wham-wham* of interceptor missiles blowing simulated attackers out of the sky.

Somehow, heaven knew how, Walter Chase managed to sneak away, inching through the packed rows of benches. As soon as the All Clear siren toots began he was up and out, ignoring the freshman warden's puppy-like yaps that they should remain in their seats until the front benches had been emptied —

Routine. It was all strictly routine.

Out on the campus, Chase headed for the airport in earnest, and was delighted to find that his flight was still on time. How lucky he was, he thought, with more pride than gratitude. 'What are you, sir?' asked the robot baggage-checker, and he said, 'Washington,' with pleasure. He was on his way. He was headed for Washington, where Dr. Hines of The Cement Research and Development Institute would assign him to his job, doubtless the first rung of a dizzying climb to wealth and fame. He was a young man on his way. Or so he thought. He did not know that he was only a neutron ambling toward events.

II

Arturo Denzer, in the same sense, was a nucleus. He knew no more about it than Walter Chase.

Denzer woke to the rays of a rising sun and the snarl of his wake-up clock. He took a vitamin capsule, an aspirin tablet, a thyroid injection; a mildly euphoric jolt of racemic amphetamine sulphate; caffeine via three cups of black coffee with sucaryl; and nicotine via a chain of non-filtering filter-tip cigarettes. He then left his apartment for the offices of *Nature's Way Magazine*, which he edited.

June's blossom was in the air, and so was the tingle of the All-Star Game Number One. The elevator operator said to him respectfully, 'Who d'ya like in the All-Star game, Mr. Denzer?' Denzer turned the operator's conversation circuit off with a handwave. He didn't feel like talking to a robot at least until the aspirin began to work.

Absent-mindedly he waved a cab to him and climbed in. Only after it took off did he notice, to his dismay, that he had picked a Black-and-White fleet hack. They were salty and picturesque – and couldn't be turned off. The damned thing would probably call him 'Mac.'

'Who ya like inna All-Star, Mac?' the cab asked genially, and Denzer winced. Trapped, he drummed his fingers on the armrest and stared at the Jefferson Memorial in its sea of amusement rides and hot-dog stands. 'Who ya like inna All-Star, Mac?' it asked again, genially and relentlessly. It would go on asking until he answered.

'Yanks,' Denzer grunted. Next time he'd watch what he was doing and get a sleek, black Rippington Livery with a respectful BBC accent.

'Them bums?' groaned the cab derisively. 'Watcha think

Craffany's up to?'

Craffany was the Yankee manager. Denzer knew that he had benched three of his star players over the last weekend – indeed, it was impossible to avoid knowing it. Denzer struck out wildly: 'Saving them for the All-Star, I guess.'

The cab grunted and said 'Maybe. My guess, Fliederwick's in a slump so Craffany benched him and pulled Hockins and Waller so it'd look like he was saving 'em for the All-Star. Ya notice Fliederwick was 0 for 11 in the first game with Navy?'

Denzer gritted his teeth and slumped down in the seat. After a moment the cab grunted and said: 'Maybe. My guess is Fliederwick's in a slump so Craffany benched him and pulled....' It went through it twice more before Denzer and his hangover could stand no more.

'I hate baseball,' he said distinctly.

The cab said at once, 'Well, it's a free country. Say, ya see Braden's speech on the C.S.B. last night?'

'I did.'

'He really gave it to them, right? You got to watch those traitors. Course, like Crockhouse says, where we going to get the money?'

'Print it, I imagine,' snarled Denzer.

'Figgers don't lie. We already got a gross national debt of $87,912.02 per person, you know that? Tack on the cost of the Civilian Shelters and whaddya got?'

Denzer's headache was becoming cataclysmic. He rubbed his temples feverishly.

'Figgers don't lie. We already got a gross national ...'

Desperate situations require desperate measures. 'I hate p-politics too,' he said, stuttering a little. Normally he didn't like smutty talk.

The cab broke off and growled: 'Watch ya language, Mac. This is a respectable fleet.'

The cab corkscrewed down to a landing in North Arlington-

Alex and said, 'Here y'are, Mac.' Denzer paid it and stepped from the windy terrace of the Press House on to a crowded westbound corridor. He hoped in a way that the cab wouldn't turn him in to a gossip columnist. In another way he didn't care.

Around him buzzed the noise of the All-Star and the C.S.B. '...Craffany ... $87,912.02, and at *least* $6,175.50 for Shelters ... Foxy Framish and Little Joe Fliederwick ... well, this *is* next year ... nah, you sneak-punch 'em a couple thousand missiles over the Pole and ... needs a year in the minors.'

'Hello, Denzer,' someone said. It was Maggie Frome, his assistant.

'Hello, Maggie,' he said, and added automatically: 'Who do you like in the All-Star game?'

In a low, ferocious voice she muttered: 'You can take the All-Star game, tie it up in a b-b-b-brassiere and dump it in a Civilian Shelter. I am sick of the subject. *Both* subjects.'

He flushed at her language and protested: 'Really, Maggie!'

'Sorry,' she grunted, sounding as though she didn't mean it. He contrasted her surly intransigence with his own reasoned remarks to the cab and tolerantly shook his head. Of course, he could have been taken the wrong way ... He began to worry.

They stepped off together at the *Nature's Way* offices. Sales & Promotion was paralyzed. Instead of rows of talkers at rows of desks, phoning prospects out of city directories and high-pressuring them into subscriptions, the department was curdled into little knots of people cheerfully squabbling about the C.S.B. and the All-Stars. Denzer sighed and led the girl on into Transmission. The gang should have been tuning up the works, ready to shoot the next issue into seven million home facsimile receivers. Instead, the gang was talking All-Stars and C.S.B. It was the same in Typography, the same in Layout, the same in Editorial.

The door closed behind them, isolating their twin office from the babble. Blessed silence. 'Maggie,' he said, 'I have a headache. Will you please work on the final paste-ups and cutting for me? There isn't anything that should give you any trouble.'

'Okay, Denzer,' she said, and retreated to her half of the office with the magazine dummy. Denzer felt a momentary pang of conscience. The issue was way overset and cutting it was a stinker of a job to pass on to Maggie Frome. Still, that was what you had assistants for, wasn't it?

He studied her, covertly, as she bent over the dummy. She was a nice-looking girl, even if she was a hangover from the administration of President Danton and his Century of the Common Woman. Maggie's mother had been something of an integrationist leader in Sandusky, Ohio, and had flocked to Washington as one mote in Danton's crackpot horde, bringing her sub-teenage daughter Maggie. No doubt there had been a father, but Maggie never mentioned him. The mother had died in a car crash that looked like suicide after Danton lost all fifty-four states in his bid for re-election, but by then Maggie was a pert teenager who moved in with cousins in Arlington-Alex and she stayed on. Must be just like Washington, Denzer thought. Not because of Female Integration, though. Danton's Century of the Common Woman had lasted just four years.

He winced a little as he remembered her coarseness of speech. She was round and brown-haired. You couldn't have everything.

Denzer leaned back and shut his eyes. The hubbub outside the office was just barely audible for a moment – some red-hot argument over the Gottshalk Committee's Shelter Report or Fliederwick's R.B.I. had swelled briefly to the shrieking stage – and then died away again. Heretically he wondered what the point was in getting excited over baseball or the building or non-building of air-raid shelters capable of housing every American all the time. One was as remote from reality as the other.

'Sorry, Denzer.'

He sat up, banging his knee on his desk.

'Lousy staff work, I'm afraid. Here's the Aztec Cocawine piece and no lab verification on the test results.' She was waving red-crayoned galleys in his face.

He looked at the scrawling red question-mark over the neat columns of type with distaste. *Nature's Way* promised its seven million subscribers that it would not sell them anything that would kill them; or, at least, that if it did kill them nobody would be able to hang it on the product directly. At substantial expense, they maintained a facility to prove this point. It was called The Nature's Way National Impartial Research Foundation. 'So call the lab,' he said.

'No good, Denzer. Front-office memo last month. Lab verifications must be *in* writing *with* notary's seal *on* hand before the issue goes to bed.'

'Cripes,' he protested, 'that means somebody's got to go clear over to Lobby House.' He did not meet her eye. Going over to Lobby House was a worthwhile break in the day's routine; the free snack-bar and free bar-bar the lobbies maintained was up to the best expense-account standards, and everyone enjoyed talking to the kooks in the lab. They were so odd.

'I'll go if you want, Denzer,' she said, startling him into looking at her.

'But the issue —'

'Did most of it last night, Denzer. The Aztec story is all that's left.'

'We'll both go,' he said, rising. She had earned it; he needed a bromo and a shot of B-1 vitagunk in the Lobby House snack-bar; and since there would be two of them in the cab he had a ruse for cutting out the cab's talk about All-Stars and the C.S.B.

The ruse was this: As soon as the cab took off he flung his arms around her and bore her back against the arm rest.

The cab chuckled and winked at them with its rear-view

lens, as it was programmed to do. They discussed proofreading, the vacation sked and the choice of lead commercials for the next issue of *Nature's Way* in soft whispers into each other's ears all the way to Lobby House, while the cab winked and chuckled at them every fifteen seconds.

The kooks on the 93d floor were under the care of a sort of half-breed race of semi-kooks. These were science majors who had minored in journalism ... or in marrying rich ... and thus wandered into press agentry for scientific concerns. As liaison men between *Nature's Way* and the test-tube manipulators the semi-kooks occupied an uncertain middle ground. It sometimes made them belligerent. Denzer and the girl were let in to see the Director of Bennington's Division, a Dr. Bennington, and Denzer said: 'We came for the Aztec Cocawine certification.'

Dr. Bennington boomed: 'Damn right! Coming right up! Say, who's gonna take it in the Game?' He thumped a button on his desk and in a moment a tall, stooped youth with a proudly beaked nose swept in and threw a document on his desk. 'Thanks, Valendora. Lessee here, um, yeah. Says it's harmless to the nerves, ya-ta-ta, ya-ta-ta, all signed and stamped. Anything else today, Arturo? Gland extract, fake a heroin prescription, shot of Scotch?'

The beaked youth said loftily: 'Our findings are set forth precisely, Dr. Bennington. The fluid contains an alkaloid which appreciably eroded the myelin sheaths of the automatic nerve trunks.'

Denzer blanched, but the semi-kook administrator agreed carelessly, 'Right, that's what I said. It's that word "appreciably." Anything less than "markedly," we write it down as negative.' He slipped it into an envelope that was already marked *Confidential Findings, Aztec Wine of Coca Corporation, Sponsor,* and sailed it across to Denzer. 'Well, what about C.S.B., boy? They gonna get us dug in before it's too late?' He made them promise to stop in at the snack-bar or bar-bar before leaving the building, then offered them a drink out of his private stock. They refused, of course. That was just his way of saying good-bye. It was the only way he knew to end a conversation.

With the certification in his pocket and the issue locked up, Denzer began to feel as though he might live, especially if he made it to the B-1 vitagunk dispenser in the snack-bar. He took Maggie Frome by the arm and was astonished to feel her shaking.

'Sorry, Denzer. I'm not crying, really. If somebody's going to sell crazy-making dope to the public, why *shouldn't* it be you and me? We're no better than anybody else, d-d-damn it!'

He said uncomfortably, 'Maybe a drink's not such a bad idea. What do you say?'

'I'd love it,' she sobbed. But then the sirens began to wail and they said, 'Damn it,' and 'Oh, dear' – respectively, she did and he did – and they took their bearings by the signs and made for the shelters. Under Lobby House was nothing like enough space, so the air-raid shelter was the interior parts of the 10th through 85th floors, away from the flying glass of the curtain walls but not too near the elevator shafts. It was not a bad shelter, actually. It was proof against any bomb that the world had ever known, up to, say, early 1943.

There was plenty of room but not enough benches. Maggie and Denzer found a place on the floor where they could put their backs against a wall, and he allowed her to lean against his shoulder. She wasn't such a bad kid, he thought sympathetically, especially as the perfume in her hair was pleasant in his nostrils. There wasn't anything really *wrong* with Female Integration. Maggie wasn't a *nut*. Take baseball. Why, that was the Integrationist's major conquest, when women demanded and got equal representation on every major-league in spite of the fact that they could not throw or run on competitive terms with men. They said that if all the teams had the same number of women it wouldn't matter. And it hadn't. And Integrationists were still crowing over the victory; and yet Maggie had refused to fall into the All-Star hysteria.

A roar like an outboard motor in the crown of your hat shook the building; A. A. 'carpet' cannon laying a sheet of sudden death for missiles across the sky above them. Denzer relaxed. His headache was almost gone. He inclined his head to rest his cheek against Maggie's hair. Even with a hangover, it had been pleasant in the cab with his arms around her. He had been kind of looking forward to the return trip. If Denzer were indeed a nucleus, as in a way he was, he was beginning to feel a certain tugging of binding energy toward certain other nuclear particles.

As soon as the noise stopped, he thought he would speak to her.

The noise stopped. The voices of the men beside them bellowed into the sudden quiet: '– damned foolish idea of Therapeutic War was exploded ten years ago! And that's what we'd be if your idiot Crockhouse was in – exploded!'

And the man next to him: 'At least Crockhouse wouldn't have us sitting in these fool imitation shelters! He'd *do* something.'

'Whadya think *Braden* wants, for God's sake? Not these things. He's right on the record for C.S.B.'

And then Maggie Frome, breathing fire, her head no longer resting on Denzer's shoulder: 'What the hell is so great about C.S.B.? Shelters, no shelters, can't you get it through your head that if this keeps up we're *dead*? Dear God above, deliver me from fools, baseball players and p-p-politicians!'

Denzer tried to look as though he'd never met her; he was white-faced. Round, yes, sweet-smelling, yes, warm – but how could he ever get used to her dirty *talk*?

III

If Denzer was a nucleus and Walter Chase, a neutron, what can we call the President of the United States? He played a part. Without him nothing could happen. Perhaps what he did was to shape the life of the neutron before fission happened; in that sense one could call him a 'moderator.' This was an apt term for President Braden.

On this bright June morning in Washington – not Arlington-Alex or the bedroom municipalities in Maryland but the little old Federal District itself – the President of the United States held what was still called a 'press' conference. He was late. The cathode-tube 'newspapermen' grumbled a little as Secret Service men frisked them, but it was habit. They were used to being frisked, ever since that fanatic Alaskan nationalist publisher emptied a ·32 at then-President Hutzmeyer in '83. And they were used to now-President Braden being late.

They rose when President Braden came in. As usual, he protested in his pleasant adopted border-South Accent: 'Please, ladies, please, gentlemen, don't bother —' So they sat down and smiled, and waited while Braden arranged some papers on his desk. He always did that. He never referred to them during the session, because he didn't have to, but every week there was the minute or two of silence in the room while the President, his rimless glasses gleaming studiously, pursed his lips over the documents in their red, blue and cream-colored folders.

He looked up and beamed.

Unobtrusive camera-eyes, mounted flush with the walls of the conference room, began to record. The elephantine Giuseppe von Bortoski, N.B.C. Washington bureau chief, incomparably senior correspondent, was privileged to lead off. He did: 'Good morning, Mr. President. Do you have a statement for us today?'

'Nothing prepared, Joseph. It's been a quiet week, hasn't it?'

Von Bortoski said solemnly, 'Not for Craffany,' and everybody roared. Von Bortoski waited out his laugh and said: 'But seriously, Mr. President, is there any comment on the radar picket situation?'

The President paused, then looked faintly surprised. 'I didn't know there was a "situation," Joseph. Our radar picket vessels off the Atlantic and Pacific coasts have been pulled in approximately two hundred miles. They all have the new microradar; they don't have to be so far out. This gives us a gratifying economy, since the closer we can pull them in the fewer ships we need to stick out there on picket duty. Is that what you wanted to know, Joseph?'

'No, Mr. President. I was referring to Representative Simpson's Telecast yesterday. He alleged that the new radars haven't been adequately field-tested. Said the move was premature and, well, dangerous.'

The President paused, then looked faintly angry. 'I seem to recall that Illinois Simpson. A Democrat.' Everybody nodded. 'I am surprised that you are taking up our time, Joseph, with the wild charges that emanate with monotonous regularity from the Party of Treason.' Everyone looked at the stout N.B.C. man with annoyance. The President turned toward a young lady correspondent, paused and said, 'Miss Bannerman, do you have a question?'

She did. What about the Civilian Shelters Bill?

The President paused, grinned and said, 'I'm for it.' He got a small laugh.

'I mean, Mr. President, what is its status now? As the leader of your Party, is it going to go through?'

The President paused longer than usual. Everyone in the room knew what he was waiting for, though it was a convention of the Press Conference to pretend he was answering off the cuff. At last the other end of the transprompter circuit got its signals cleared and the President said levelly: 'As the leader of my Party, Miss Bannerman, I can say this thing is being hammered out. Slower than some of us would wish, true. But it will be done. It is the platform of my Party; on that platform I was elected in '98; and I have not the reputation of going back on my pledges.' He inclined his head to an approving stir among the correspondents.

Von Bortoski made a mental calculation. He decided that the press conference had supplied enough matter for his upcoming newscast and to hell with the rest of them. 'Thank you, Mr. President,' he said. The other reporters swore under their breaths once more at the tyranny of the senior-correspondent rule, the President rose smiling and the armed guards stepped away from the doors.

C.S.B., C.S.B., the President meditated. Some day he would have to ask a question himself and find out just what this C.S.B. was all about. No doubt the R & I desk that fed him answers or speeches via the transprompter could tell him. He promised himself he would get around to it first thing, say, Monday. Or wait, wasn't Monday the first All-Star game?

A swift conveyor belt whisked him from the Annex to the Old White House and an escalator to the Oval Room. His personal secretary ventured to say: 'You made good time, Governor. There's thirty-five minutes clear before the first appointment. How about a nap?'

President Braden snapped: 'I see General Standish has been talking to you again, Murray. Tell that quack when I want doctoring I'll ask for it, and get me a drink.'

The President, who liked to think he was a hard-riding, hard-drinking southern gentleman, although he had been a New Jersey accountant until he was thirty, sipped a glass of mineral water lightly tinted with whisky, decided he was refreshed and buzzed for the first appointment to start ahead of time.

The first appointment was with Senator Horton of Indiana. While he was coming in the transprompter whispered into the President's ear: 'Call him David, not Dave. No wife. Ex-professor, for God's sake. Watch him.'

The President rose, smiling, and gripped Horton's hand with warmth and the pressure of an old campaigner. 'It's a great pleasure, David. How's Indiana shaping up for next year? Lose all your best seniors?'

Senator Horton had a shock of gray hair, a mournful face and a surprisingly springy, lean body for a fifty-year-old ex-professor. He said abruptly: 'I don't follow the school's football schedule. Mr. President, I want something.'

'Unto the half of my kingdom,' Braden said gaily, attempting to throw him off balance.

Horton gave him a meager smile. 'I want you to bear down on the Civilian Shelters Bill. You are, after all, committed to it. It helped elect you. But twenty-two months have gone by and the bill is still in the Public Works Committee. I am on that committee, Mr. President, and it is my impression that I am the only member interested in seeing it enacted into law.'

The President said gravely, 'That's a mighty serious charge, David. One, I cannot act on without the fullest —'

'Excuse me for interrupting, Mr. President, but your time is valuable and there are some things you needn't bother explaining to me.' Deeply affronted, the President stared at him. 'Believe me when I say that I've come to you as a last resort. I get only bland evasions from Harkness. The Interior Department —'

Harkness was the committee chairman and he had been Braden's personal campaign manager in the '96 run. The President rose and said, 'Excuse *me*, Senator, but I don't permit people to speak about Jim Harkness like that in my presence.'

Senator Horton distractedly ran his hands through his shock of hair. 'I didn't mean to offend you. God knows I don't mean to offend anyone. Not even the Secretary of Interior, though if he thinks — No, I won't say that. All I want is to get the C.S.B. on the floor and get the construction work under way. Mr. President, how long can all this go on?'

The President remained standing, looked at his watch and said coolly, 'All what, David?'

'We are in the fifty-third year of the Political War, Mr. President. Somehow, by a succession of last-minute, hairsbreadth accidents, we have escaped nuclear bombing. It can't go on forever! If the missiles came over the Pole today they'd annihilate this nation, and I don't give one juicy damn that China and Russia would be annihilated in the next forty minutes —'

He was trembling. The President's earphone whispered tinnily: 'Hospitalized one year; nervous breakdown. The guard-ports have him covered with sleep guns, sir.' That was a relief; but what about this Horton? He was Doane's personal choice, chairman of the National Committee; had Doane put a raving maniac in the Senate? The President remembered, from those young, county-committeeman days when he remembered things clearly, that something like that had happened before. It had been during the Party of Treason's first years – a lunatic from the Northwest got elected to Congress and was mighty embarrassing until he committed suicide. The President, then a schoolboy, had chuckled with the rest of the nation over Congressman Zioncheck; but now he was not chuckling. It was *his* Administration and in the *Senate*. And a member of, God help him, *his* party.

The President did not look toward the guard-ports and the riflemen behind them. He said quietly, 'David, I want you to calm down. No pledges have been forgotten and no pledges are going to be violated. I'll speak to Jim Harkness about the Shelter Bill today. That's a promise.'

'Thank you,' Horton said gratefully, and tried to smile. 'I'll hold you to that, sir. Good day.'

The President buzzed, not for his next appointment but to talk to his secretary. 'Murray, get me Senator Harkness on the phone.' And to his chest microphone: 'Transprompter desk? Get out of circuit. I'll buzz you.' He heard the faint carrier tone in his ear die and the guard-ports' click. For the first time since he stepped out of his shower that morning, the President was able to say a word that no one but himself could hear. He said it. It had only one syllable, but it improved his mood very much.

Harkness's voice was resonant and comforting. The President, sometimes nagged by a secret feeling that he was not very bright, knew damned well that he was brighter than Harkness.

He said: 'Jim, I've got to wondering about this C.S.B. that you've got in Public Works. The day's young yet and I've had two questions about it. I know we campaigned on it – what is it, exactly?'

Harkness said comfortingly: 'It's under control, Brad. That fellow Horton is trying to unbottle it, but we can keep him quiet. He doesn't know the ropes.'

'Know that, Jim. I just had him in here, wailing and mad. What's it all about?'

'Why,' said Senator Harkness, with something less of assurance in his voice, 'it's about building shelters, Brad. Against nuclear attack.' He pronounced it 'nookyoular,' in the approved White House fashion.

'Not quite my point, Jim. I mean' — the President searched for what it was he did mean – 'I mean, I can find out the facts and so on, but what's got people so stirred up? Put it this way, Jim: What's your philosophy about the Civilian Shelters Bill?'

'Philosophy?' Harkness sounded vaguely scared. 'Well, I would not know about philosophy, Brad. It's an issue, C.S.B. is, and we're very fortunate to have got it away from the Nationalists. C.S.B.'s very popular.' The President sighed inaudibly and relaxed; Senator Harkness was clearly about to launch into one of his famous explanations of things that never needed to be explained. 'You see, Brad, an issue is lifeblood to a party. Look over the field today. What's to argue about? Damn little. Everybody knows the Party of Treason is the Party of Treason. Everybody knows the Commies are crazy hoodlums, can't trust 'em. Everybody knows atomic re-

taliation is the only sound military policy. There, at one
sweep, you knock domestic, foreign and military policy off the
board and haven't anything left to play with except C.S.B.' He
paused for breath, but before the President could try to get
him back on the track of the question he was rushing on: 'It's
a godsend, Brad! The Nationalists guessed wrong. They
turned C.S.B. down in the name of economy. My opinion,
they listened too much to the Defense Department people;
naturally the generals didn't want to admit they can't intercept
whatever the Commies throw at us, and naturally they want
the money for interception instead of shelters. Well, that's all
right, too, but the people say the last word. We Middle-
Roaders guessed right. We slapped C.S.B. in our platform,
and we won. What else is there to say about it? Now, we're
not going to turn loose of an issue like that. Fools if we did.
The strategy's to milk it along, get it on the floor just before
we adjourn for campaign trips and if a Nationalist filibuster
kills it, so much the better. That saves it for us for next year!
You know, you never get credit in this game for what you've
done. Only for what you're going to do. And, *hell*, Brad,' he
crowed, suddenly exultant as a child who has found a dime in
the street, 'this thing is good for years! There has to be a big
conference committee with the House on financing C.S.B., we
haven't even set up liaison with Military Affairs. We've got
four more years easy. How's that sound, Brad, eh? Ride right
in to re-election in Twenty Oh Oh, the first President of the
twenty-first century!'

'Thanks, Jim,' said the President, 'I knew I could get a
straight answer out of you.' It was the only way to stop him.
Otherwise he might go clear on to the C.S.B. and its effect on
the Integrationists, the C.S.B. and Labor, the C.S.B. and
Colorado water diversion or the C.S.B. as viewed in the light
of Craffany's benching of Little Joe Fliederwick.
     And yet, pondered the President, he still didn't know even
the question, much less the answer. *Why* was C.S.B. a good

issue? The missiles hadn't hit in the past 53 years, why should a voting population march to the booths and elect its leaders because of their Shelter philosophy now?

Braden changed the subject. 'What do you think of Horton, Jim?'

He could always count on Harkness being frank, at least. 'Don't like him. A boat-rocker. You want my advice, Brad? You haven't asked for it, but it's get rid of him. Get the National Committee to put a little money in his district before the primaries.'

'I see,' said the President, thanked his former campaign manager and hung up.

He took a moment before buzzing Murray for the next appointment to sip his lightly tinted soda-water and close his eyes. Well, he'd wasted most of the thirty-five minutes he'd gained, and not even a nap to show for it. Maybe General Standish was right.

Once when Braden was younger, before he was governor of New Jersey, before he was state senator, when he still lived in the old Rumford house on the beach and commuted to Jersey City every day – once he had been a member of the National Guard, what he considered his obligation as a resigned West Pointer. And they had killed two of their obligatory four-hours-a-month one month watching a documentary film on nuclear attack. The arrows marched over the Pole and the picture dissolved to a flight of missiles. The warheads, exploded high in air. Then the film went to stock shots, beautifully selected and paced: the experimental houses searing and burning on Yucca Flats, the etched shadows of killed men on the walls of Hiroshima, a forest fire, a desert, empty, and the wind lifting sand-devils. The narration had told how such-and-such kind of construction would be burned within so-many miles of Ground Zero. It remarked that forest fires would blaze on every mountain and mentioned matter-of-factly that they wouldn't go out until the winter snow or spring rains, and of course then the ground would be bare and the top soil would creep as mud down to the oceans. It estimated that then, the year was no later than 1960, a full-scale attack would cost the world ninety per cent of its capacity to support life for at least a couple of centuries. Braden had never forgotten that movie.

He had never forgotten it, but he admitted that sometimes he had allowed it to slip out of his mind for a while. This latest while seemed to have lasted quite a few years. Only C.S.B. had brought it back in his recollection.

Because that was the question, the President thought, sipping his tinted soda-water. What was the use of C.S.B.? What was the use of any kind of shelters, be they deep as damn-all, if all you had to come out of them to was a burned-out Sahara?

IV

Now that the simulated raid was over, everybody was resuming their interrupted errands at once. Denzer was crammed in any-which-way with Maggie Frome wedged under an arm and that kook from the Institute – Venezuela? – gabbling in his ear about computer studies and myelin sheaths.

The elevator jollied them all along. 'Don't forget tomorrow, folks. Be a lot of grandmothers buried tomorrow, eh?' It could not wink, but it giggled and, well, nudged them. Or at least it shook them. It was overloaded with the crowds from the shelter floors, and its compensators flagged, dropping it an inch below the sill of the lobby door, then lifting it. 'Sorry, folks,' it apologized. 'Good night, all!'

Denzer grabbed Maggie's arm. The laboratory man called after him, but he only nodded and tugged the girl away through the crowds, which were mumbling to each other: 'Foxy Framish ... slip 'em a couple thousand nookyoular ... caught off first ... oh, hell.' The 'oh, hells' became general as they reached the main lobby outside of the elevator bays.

Civilian Air Wardens formed chains across the exits. Like fish weirs they chuted the excited civilians into lines and passed each line through a checkpoint.

'Denzer,' groaned Maggie, 'I'm cooked. I *never* wear my dosimeter badge with this old green dress.'

The wardens were checking every person for his compulsory air-raid equipment. Denzer swore handily, then brightened. They did have their press cards; this *was* official business. Aztec Wine of Coca was a powerful name in industry, and didn't they have a right to take care of its affairs even if they overlooked a few formalities that nobody really took very seriously anyway? He said confidently: 'Bet I get us out of it, Maggie. Watch this.' And he led her forcefully to the nearest warden. 'You there. Important morale business; here's my card. I'm Denzer of *Nature's Way*. This's my assistant, Frome. I —'

Briskly the warden nodded. 'Yes, *sir*, Mr. Denzer. Just come this way.' He led them through the purse-seine of wardens, out of the building, into – why, Denzer saw, outraged, into a *police cab*.

'You fixed us fine, Denzer,' gloomed Maggie at his side as they got in. He didn't have the spirit to listen to her.

The roundup had bagged nearly fifty hardened criminals, like Denzer and Maggie, caught flagrantly naked of dosimeters and next-of-kin tags. They were a surly lot. Even the C.S.B. adherents among them belligerently protested their treatment; the sneak-punchers were incandescent about the whole thing. Office girls, executives, errand boys, even one hangdog A.R.P. guard himself; they were a motley assortment. The research man, Valendora, was among them, and so was the girl from the Institute's reception room. Valendora saw Denzer and slipped through the crowd toward him, holding a manila envelope as though it contained diphtheria vaccine and he was the first man to arrive at the scene of an epidemic. 'Mr. Denzer,' he said darkly, 'I ask you to assist me. Eleven months of my time and twenty-two computer hours! And this is the only copy. *Statist. Analysis Trans.* expects this by tomorrow at the latest, and —'

Denzer hardly heard. *Statist. Analysis Trans.* was not the only periodical expecting something from one of the fish in this net. With an inner ear Denzer was listening to what his Front Office would say. He was, he saw clearly, about to miss a deadline. Seven million paid-up subscribers would be complaining to the Front Office when their copies were late, and Denzer knew all too well who Front Office would complain to about *that*. He whimpered faintly and reached for an amphetamine tablet, but an A.R.P. cop caught his arm. 'Watch it, Mac,' said the cop, not unkindly. 'No getting rid of evidence there. You got to turn all that stuff in.'

Denzer had never been arrested before. He was in a semi-daze while they were waiting to be booked. Ahead of him in line a minor squabble arose — Valendora seemed to be clashing with a plump young fellow in a collegiate crew-cut — but Denzer was paying little attention as he numbly emptied his pockets and put all his possessions on the desk to be locked away for him.

It was not until Maggie Frome repeated his name for the fifth time that he realized she was talking to him. She indicated a lanky, homely woman talking into an autonoter, seemingly on terms of amiable mutual contempt with the police.

'Denzer,' Maggie hissed urgently, 'that girl over there. The reporter. Name's Sue-Mary Gribb, and I know her. Used to work with her on the *Herald*.'

'That's nice. Say, Maggie,' he moaned, 'what the devil are we going to do about the Aztec Wine of Coca piece? The Front Office'll have our heads.'

'What I'm trying to tell you. Denzer! Give her the lab report. She'll take it in for us!'

The sun rose in pink glory for Arturo Denzer.

Half blinded by the radiance of sudden, unexpected hope, he staggered back to the desk. Valendora and the plump youth were still at it, but he pushed past them, picked up the Nature's Way National Impartial Research Foundation envel-

ope and clawed his way back to Maggie. 'Pencil!' he snapped.
She produced one and Denzer scribbled a note to Joe, in Production:

> Joe, we're in a jam. Fix this up for us somehow. Run it
> pp 34–35, push it through soonest, I've already got all okays
> so just jam it in. God bless you. If Front Office asks where I
> am I'm dead.

He thought of adding, 'Will explain later,' but he wasn't so
very sure he could. He thought of kissing Sue-Mary Gribb;
but she was another Female Integrationist, wearing slacks,
carrying a corncob pipe; he only shook her hand briskly and
watched her leave.

It was not until she was out the door that he realized why
she had been there in the first place.

She was a reporter, gathering names. It was customary to
run a list of A.R.P. violators in the newspapers. It was inevitable that someone who worked for *Nature's Way* would see his
and Maggie's names on that list; and it was beyond hope that
that someone would fail to show it to the Front Office.

With the help of Sue-Mary Gribb he might have made his
deadline, but his troubles were not over. Front Office was solid
C.S.B.

'Maggie,' he said faintly, 'when you left the *Herald*, did you
part friends? I mean, do you think they might give us a job?'

The next thing was that they had to wait for their hearing and,
in the way of police courts, that took some time. Meanwhile
they were all jammed together, noisy and fretful.

The bull-pen roared 'Quiet down, you mokes! You think
this is a debating society?' Denzer sighed and changed position slightly so as not to disturb Maggie Frome, again placidly
dozing on his shoulder. (This could become a habit, he
thought.)

Well, that was something else the Century of the Common

Woman had accomplished. They had integrated the lockups, for better or for worse. Not that Maggie, asleep, was deriving the benefit she might from the integrated, but still very loud, yammering of the inmates of the bull-pen.

They weren't all A.R.P. violators. A sizeable knot in one corner were clearly common drunks, bellowing about the All-Star Game when they were not singing raucously. They were the chief targets of the bull-pen's repeated thunderings for quiet, as its volumetric ears registered an excessive noise level. They must wear out those tapes in a week, Denzer thought.

A diffident finger touched his arm. 'Mr. Denzer?' It was the research fellow from the Institute.

Softly, to refrain from disturbing Maggie, he said: 'Hello, Venezuela. Make yourself comfortable.'

'Valendora, Mr. Denzer.'

'Sorry,' said Denzer absently, inhaling Maggie's hair.

'I ask you, Mr. Denzer,' Valendora said, choosing his words with as much care as though he were taping a question for his computers, 'is it proper that I should be arrested for being twenty-six feet away from where I would not be arrested?'

Denzer stared at him. 'Come again?' Maggie stirred restlessly on his shoulder.

'I was two floors below the Foundation, Mr. Denzer, no more,' said the research man. 'We are not required to wear dosimeters in the Institute itself. Two floors is twenty-six feet.'

Denzer sighed. This was not a time when he had patience for nuts. The girl on his shoulder stirred and he said, 'Good morning, Maggie.' Valendora swept on:

'Naturally, Mr. Denzer, it did not occur to me to go back for my dosimeter. My probable error was more than twenty-four hours minus, though zero plus, and it might have been the real attack. I was carrying a most important document and I could not endanger it.'

Maggie looked at him with faint curiosity and then twisted

around to look at Denzer's face. 'The deadline, Denzer?' she muttered. He crossed his fingers and shrugged.

'Mr. Denzer,' cried Valendora, 'you are a man of influence. *Statist. Analysis Trans.* is waiting for this study – and besides,' he added wonderingly, 'I suppose, if the attack is to come tomorrow someone should do something about it. Can you not secure justice for me in this matter?'

Rocked by the sudden vision of himself as a man of influence, Denzer hardly heard the rest of what the research man was saying. Maggie Frome pushed herself away from him and stared thoughtfully at Valendora.

'We're all in the same boat, friend,' she said kindly.

Valendora scowled at the floor.

'But what's this about an attack?'

With bitter sarcasm Valendora said, 'Nothing at all, Miss Frome. Merely what I have spent eleven months of my time on. *And* twenty-two computer hours.'

'I'm impressed, friend. You said something about an attack?'

Valendora said, 'You would not understand single-event prediction, Miss Frome. It is a statistical assessment of probabilities. Oh, nothing in itself that has not previously been studied, true; but it is in the establishing of quantitative values for subjective data that I have, I do know, made a contribution.' He shrugged moodily. 'And by tomorrow? The event, you see. If I have not published before the event it is only a mathematical statement. The test of a theory is the predictions that can be made from it; I have made my prediction. During the All-Star Game, you see —'

'There you are!' cried a new voice.

It was the plump youth who had been quarrelling with Valendora at the booking desk. He was still angry. 'Baseball,' he snapped, 'that's all I hear. Can't I make anyone understand that I am a special investigator on Senator Horton's *personal* staff? The senator is waiting to interview me right now! And this man has stolen my thesis!' He put a hand out and briskly pumped Denzer's. 'Walter Chase, sir. M.A., C.E., and all the rest of that nonsense,' he twinkled, for he had made a quick estimate of Denzer's well-cut clothes and hangdog look and pigeonholded him at once as *second-string executive, subject to flattery.*

'Denzer. *Nature's Way*,' he mumbled, trying to let go of the hand, but Chase hung on.

'I'm in cement, Mr. Denzer,' he said. 'Did a bit of research – my dissertation, actually – just received another degree – and Senator Horton is most taken by it. Most taken, Mr. Denzer. Unfortunately I've just the one copy, as it happens and it's, well, rather important that it not be lost. It concerns cement, as it affects our shelter program – and, after all, what *is* a shelter but cement? Eh? Probably should've been classified at the start, but —' He shrugged with the faint amused distaste of the man of science for the bureaucrat. 'Anyway, I must have it; the senator must see it with his own eyes before he'll give me the j – before making final arrangements. And this man has stolen it.'

'Stolen!' screamed Valendora. 'Man! It is your fault, man! I was only —'

'Be careful!' commanded Chase furiously. 'Don't blame *me*! I was merely —'

Danzer felt a tug on his arm. Maggie Frome winked and led him away, near the group of singing drunks. They sat down again. 'Quieter here!' she shouted in his ear. 'Put your shoulder back, Denzer! I want to go back to sleep!'

'All right!' he yelled, and helped her settle her head against him; but in a moment she raised it again.

'Denzer!' she asked over the singing of the group, 'did you hear what your friend from the Institute was saying? Something about an attack? I had the funny idea he meant missile attack – a real one, I mean.'

'No,' he shouted back, 'it was only baseball! All-Star Game, you know.'

And he hardly heard the raucous bellowing of the drunks for the next half hour, inhaling the fragrance of her hair.

They were released at last, Denzer making bail; the bail corresponded to the amount of their fines for A.R.P. violation, and small print at the bottom of their summons pointed out that they could forfeit it if they chose, thus paying their fines, simply by failing to appear at the magistrate's trial. They got out just in time to get the bulldog edition of *Nature's Way* from a sidewalk scriber.

They looked at once on the spread, pages 34 and 35, expecting anything, even blank pages.

Tragically, the pages were not blank at all.

Pages 34 and 35 had nothing to do with Aztec Wine of Coca. It was a straight news story, headlined:

U. S. MISSILE VULNERABILITY TOTAL IN ALL-STAR GAME, SAYS GOVERNMENT STATISTICS EXEPERT

From there it got worse. Maggie screamed faintly over Denzer's shoulder as she read parts of it aloud: ' "The obsessive preoccupation of the American public with baseball stems from a bread-and-circuses analogy with ancient Rome. Now, as then, it may lead to our destruction." Denzer! Does this maniac want us to get lynched?'

'Read on,' moaned Denzer, already several laps ahead of her. Neatly boxed on the second page was a digested, sexed-up version of something Denzer recognized faintly as the study of cement in the shelter program Chase had mentioned. What the *Nature's Way* semantic-digester had made of it was:

SHELTER DEATH TRAPS

Study of the approved construction codes of all American shelter projects indicates that they will not withstand even large chemical explosives.

'I think,' sobbed Arturo Denzer, 'that I'll cut my throat.'

'Not here, Mac,' snapped the news-scribing machine. 'Move on, will you? *Hey!* Late! Whaddya read?'

Shaking, the couple moved on. 'Denzer,' Maggie gasped, 'where do you think Joe got this stuff?'

'Why, from us, Maggie.' Denzer tried to swallow, but his throat was dry. 'Didn't you hear Chase before? That was the mix-up at the desk; we must have got his papers, and I suppose what's hisname's, Venezuela's, and bundled them off to Joe. Nice job of rush typography, though,' he added absently, staring into space. 'Say, Maggie. What Venezuela was talking about. You think there's any truth to it?'

'To what, Denzer?'

'What it says here. Optimum time for the Other Side to strike – during the All-Star Game, it says. You think—?'

Maggie shook her head. 'I don't think, Denzer,' she said, and they walked on for a moment.

They heard their names called, turned, and were overtaken rapidly by Valendora and the cement engineer. 'You!' cried Chase. 'You have my thesis!'

'And you have my study!' cried Valendora.

'Not I but humanity,' said Denzer sadly, holding out the damp faxed edition of *Nature's Way*.

Valendora, after one white-faced oath in Spanish, took it calmly. He glanced up at the sky for a second, then shrugged. 'Someone will not like this. I should estimate,' he said thoughtfully, 'that within five minutes we will all be back in the *calabozo*.'

But he was wrong.

It was actually less than three.

V

It was the third inning, and Craffany had just benched Little Joe Fliederwick. In spite of the sudden ban on air travel the stadium was full. Every television screen in the country followed Little Joe's trudging walk to the dugout.

In the White House, President Braden, shoes off, sipping a can of beer, ignored the insistent buzzing in his ear as long as he could. He wanted to watch the game. '– and the crowd is *roaring*,' roared the announcer, 'just a-*boiling*, folks! What's Craffany up to? What will he do next? Man, don't we have one going here *today*? Folks, was that the all-important turning point in today's all-im – in today's record-breaking All-Star Game, folks? Well, we'll see. In sixty seconds we'll return to the field, but meanwhile —'

The President allowed his attention to slip away from the commercial and took another pull at his beer. Baseball, now. That was something he could get his teeth into. He'd been a fan since the age of five. All his life. Even during the Century of the Common Woman, when that madman Danton had listened to the Female Lobby and put girls on every second base in the nation. But it had never been this good. This Fliederwick, now, he was *good*.

Diverted, he glanced at the screen. The camera was on Little Joe again, standing at the steps to the dugout, looking up. So were his teammates; and the announcer was saying: 'Looks like some more of those air-to-air missile-busters, folks. A huge flight of them. *Way* up. Well, it's good to know our country's defense is being looked after and, say, speaking of defense, what do you suppose Craffany's going to do now that —'

The buzzing returned. The President sighed and spoke to his invisible microphones. 'What? Oh. Well, damn it ... all right.'

With a resentful heart he put down the beer can and snapped off the television set. He debated putting his shoes back on. He decided against it, and pulled his chair close to the desk to hide his socks.

The door opened and Senator Horton came in.

'Mr. President,' cried Horton, 'I want to thank you. There's no doubt your prompt action has saved your country, sir. I imagine you've been filled in on the, ah, incident.'

Well, he had been, the President thought, but by Senator Harkness, and maybe the time had come when Jim Harkness' view of world affairs needed a little broadening. 'Suppose you tell me about it,' he said.

Horton looked faintly perplexed, but said promptly: 'It was basically an accident. Two men, working independently, came up with reports, strictly unofficial, but important. One was a graduate student's thesis on shelter construction; happens the boy was looking for a job, the Cement Research & Development Institute recommended him to me, he was on his way to see me when the thing happened. That's how I became involved in it. The other fellow's a lab worker, at least as far as earning a living's concerned, but he's a mathematician something-or-other and was working out a problem with his lab's computers. The problem: If the Reds are going to sneak-punch us, when will they do it? The answer: today. While we're all off base, with the All-Star Game. In the old days they'd maybe pick a presidential election to put one over, just like Hitler used to pick the long weekends. Now all they need is a couple of hours when everybody's looking the other way, you see. All-Star Game's a natural.'

The President said mildly, 'I can see that without using a computer, Senator.'

'Certainly, sir. But this boy proved it. Like to meet him, by the way? I've got the lot of them, right outside.'

In for a penny, in for a pound, thought the President, motioning them in. There were three men and a girl, rather young, rather excited. Senator Horton rattled off introductions. The President gathered the other two had been involved in the security leak that had occurred on the reports.

'But I've talked to them,' cried Senator Horton, 'and I can't believe there's a grain of malice in all of them. And what they say, Mr. President, requires immediate action.'

'I was under the impression I'd taken immediate action,'

said the President. 'You asked me to ground all civilian air traffic so the missile-watchers could have a clear field; I did. You asked me to put all our defense aircraft airborne; I did. You asked for a Condition Red defense posture and you got it, all but the official announcement.'

'Yes, Mr. President. The immediate danger may have been averted, yes. But what about the future?'

'I see,' said the President, and paused for a second. Oddly, there was no voice from the prompter in his ear to suggest his next words. He frowned.

'I see,' he said again, louder. The tiny voice in his ear said at last:

'Well, sir, uh —' It cleared its throat. 'Sir, there seems to be some confusion here. Perhaps you could ask the Senator to continue to brief you.'

'Well —' said the President.

'David,' whispered the prompter.

'— David, let's get our thinking organized. Why don't you continue to fill me in?'

'Gladly, sir! As you know, I'm Shelters all the way. Always have been. But what this young man here says has shaken me to the core. Mr. Venezuela says —' Valendora grinned sullenly at the rug — 'that at this very moment we would be in atoms if it hadn't been for his timely publication of the statistical breakdown of our vulnerability. He's even a little sore about it, Mr. President.'

'Sore?'

The senator grinned. 'We spoiled his prediction,' he explained. 'Of course, we saved our own lives ... The Other Side has computers too; they must have assessed our national preoccupation with baseball. Beyond doubt they intended to strike. Only the commotion his article caused – not only in our own country but, through their embassies, on the Other Side – plus of course your immediate reaction when I telephoned you asking for a Red Alert, kept the missiles from coming down today, sir. I'm certain of it. And this other young fellow, Mr.

Chase —' Walter Chase bowed his head modestly — 'brought out a lot of data in his term paper, or whatever it was. Seemed like nonsense, sir, so we checked it. Everything he said is not only fact but old stuff; it's been published hundreds of times. Not a word of new material in it.' Chase glared. 'That's why we've never built deep shelters. They simply won't stand up against massive attack — and cannot be made to stand up. It's too late for shelters. In building them we're falling into the oldest strategic trap of human warfare: We're fighting yesterday's war today.'

President Braden experienced a sinking feeling when the earprompter said only, and doubtfully, 'Ask him to go on, sir.'

'Go on, si – Go on, David.'

'Why,' said the senator, astonished, 'that's all there is, Mr. President. The rest is up to you.'

President Braden remembered vaguely, as a youth, stories about the administration of President – who was it? Truman, or somebody around then. They said Truman had a sign on his desk that read: *The buck stops here.*

His own desk, the President noticed for the first time, was mirror-smooth. It held no such sign. Apart from the framed picture of his late wife there was nothing.

Yet the principle still held, remorselessly, no matter how long he had been able to postpone its application. He was the last man in the chain. There was no one to whom the President could pass the buck. If it was time for the nation to pick itself up, turn itself round and head off in a new direction, he was the only one who could order it to march.

He thought about the alternatives. Say these fellows were right. Say the shelters couldn't keep the nation going in the event of allout attack. Say the present alert, so incredibly costly in money and men, could not be maintained around the clock for any length of time, which it surely could not. Say the sneak-punchers were right ...

But no, thought the President somberly, that avenue had

been explored and the end was disaster. You could never get *all* the opposing missile bases, not while some were under the sea and some were touring the highways of the Siberian tundra on trucks and some were orbital and some were airborne. And it only took a handful of survivors to kill you.

So what was left?

Here and now, everybody was waiting for him to speak – even the little voice in his ear.

The President pushed his chair back and put his feet up on the desk. 'You know,' he said, wiggling his toes in their Argyle socks, 'I once went to school too. True,' he said, not apologizing, 'it was West Point. That's a good school too, you know. I remember writing a term paper in one of the sociology courses ... or was it history? No matter. I still recall what I said in that paper. I said wasn't it astonishing that things always got worse before they got better. Take monarchy, I said. It built up and up, grew more complex, more useless, more removed from government, in any real sense, until we come to things like England's Wars of the Roses and France's Sun King and the Czar and the Mikado – until most of the business of the government was in the person of the king, instead of the other way around. Then – bang! No more monarchy.'

'Mr. President,' whispered the voice in his ear, 'you have an appointment with the Mongolian Legate.'

'Oh, shut up, you,' said the President amiably, shocking his prompter and confusing his guests. 'Sorry, not you,' he apologized. 'My, uh, secretary. Tells me that the Chinese representatives want to talk about our "unprecedented and unpeace-loving acts" – more likely, to see what they can find out.' He picked the plug out of his ear and dropped it into a desk drawer. 'They'll wait. Now, take slavery,' he went on. 'It too became more institutionalized – and ritualized – until the horse was riding the man; until the South here was existing on slaves, it was even existing for slaves. The biggest single item of wealth in the thirteen Confederate states was slaves. The biggest single line of business, other than agriculture, was slavery, dealing and breeding. Things get big and formal, you see, just before they pop and blow away. Well, I wrote all this up. I turned it in, real proud, expecting, I don't know, maybe an honorary LL.D At least a compliment, certainly ... It came back and the instructor had scrawled one word across the top of it *Toynbee*. So I read up on Toynbee's books. After, of course, I got over being oppressed at the instructor's injustice to me. He was right. Toynbee described the whole thing long before I did.

'But, you know, I didn't know that at the time. I thought it up myself, as if Toynbee had never lived,' said the President with some pride. He beamed at them.

Senator Horton was standing with open mouth. He glanced quickly at the others in the room, but they had nothing but puzzlement to return to him. He said, 'Mr. President, I don't understand. You mean—'

'Mean? I mean what's happened to us,' said the President testily. 'We've had our obsessive period. Now we move on to something else. And, Senator, Congress is going to have to help move; and, I'm warning you, you're going to help me move *it*.'

When they left the White House it was late afternoon. The lilacs that bordered the wall were in full, fragrant bloom. Denzer inhaled deeply and squeezed the hand of Maggie Frome.

Passing the sentry box at the end of the drive, they heard a voice from a portable radio inside. It was screaming:

'It's going ... it's *going* ... it's GONE, folks! Craffany has pulled one out of the fire again! And that wraps it up for him, as Hockins sends one *way* out over center-field and into the stands...' The guard looked out, rosily beaming, and waved them on. He would have waved them on if they had worn beards and carried ticking bombs; he was a Craffany rooter from way back, and now in an ecstasy of delight.

'Craffany did it, then,' said Walter Chase sagely. 'I *thought* when he benched Hockins and moved Little Joe Fliederwick to —'

'Oh, shut up, Chase,' said Denzer. 'Maggie, I'm buying drinks. You want to come along, Venezuela?'

'I think not, Mr. Denzer,' said the research man. 'I'm late now. *Statist. Analysis Trans.* is expecting me.'

'Chase?' Politeness forced that one out of him. But Chase shook his head.

'I just remembered an old friend here in town,' said Chase. He had had time for some quick thinking. If the nation was going over to a non-shelter philosophy — if cave-dwelling was at an end and a dynamic new program was going to start — maybe a cement degree wasn't going to be the passport to security and fame he had imagined. Walter Chase had always had a keen eye for the handwriting on the wall. 'A young lady friend,' he winked. 'Name of Douglasina Baggett. Perhaps you've heard of her father; he's quite an important man in H. E. & W.'

The neutron, properly placed, had struck the nucleus; and the spreading chain was propagating rapidly through their world. What was it going to be from now on? They did not know; does a fissioned atom know what elements it will change into? It *must* change; and so it changes. 'I guess we did something, eh?' said Denzer. 'But ... I don't know. If it hadn't been us, I expect it would have been someone else. Something had to give.' For it doesn't matter which nucleus fissions first. Once the mass is critical the chain reaction begins; it is as simple as that.

'Let's get that drink, Denzer,' said Maggie Frome.

They flagged a cab, and all the way out to Arlington-Alex it chuckled at them as they kissed. The cab spared them its canned thoughts, and that was as they wished it. But that was not why they were in each other's arms.

Elphen DeBeckett lay dying. It was time. He had lived in the world for one hundred and nine years, though he had seen little enough of it except for the children. The children, thank God, still came. He thought they were with him now: 'Coppie,' he whispered in a shrivelled voice, 'how nice to see you.' The nurse did not look around, although she was the only person in the room besides himself, and knew that he was not addressing her.

The nurse was preparing the injections the doctor had ordered her to have ready. This little capsule for shock, this to rally his strength, these half-dozen others to shield him from his pain. Most of them would be used. DeBeckett was dying in a pain that once would have been unbearable and even now caused him to thresh about sometimes and moan.

DeBeckett's room was a great twelve-foot chamber with hanging drapes and murals that reflected scenes from his books. The man himself was tiny, gnomelike. He became even less material while death (prosey biology, the chemistry of colloids) drew inappropriately near his head. He had lived his life remote from everything a normal man surrounds himself with. He now seemed hardly alive enough to die.

DeBeckett lay in a vast, pillared bed, all the vaster for the small burden he put on it, and the white linen was whiter for his merry brown face. 'Darling Veddie, please don't cry,' he whispered restlessly, and the nurse took up a hypodermic syringe. He was not in unusual pain, though, and she put it back and sat down beside him.

The world had been gentle with the gentle old man. It had made him a present of this bed and this linen, this great house with its attendant horde of machines to feed and warm and comfort him, and the land on which stood the tiny, quaint houses he loved better. It had given him a park in the mountains, well stocked with lambs, deer and birds of blazing, spectacular color, a fenced park where no one ever went but DeBeckett and the beloved children, where earthmoving machines had scooped out a Very Own Pond ('My Very Own Pond/Which I sing for you in this song/Is eight Hippopotamuses Wide/And twenty Elephants Long.') He had not seen it for years, but he knew it was there. The world had given him, most of all, money, more money than he could ever want. He had tried to give it back (gently, hopefully, in a way pathetically), but there was always more. Even now the world showered him with gifts and doctors, though neither could prevail against the stomping pitchfire arsonist in the old man's colon. The disease, a form of gastroenteritis, could have been cured; medicine had come that far long since. But not in a body that clung so lightly to life.

He opened his eyes and said strongly, 'Nurse, are the children there?'

The nurse was a woman of nearly sixty. That was why she had been chosen. The new medicine was utterly beyond her in theory, but she could follow directions; and she loved Elphen DeBeckett. Her love was the love of a child, for a thumbed edition of *Coppie Brambles* had brightened her infancy. She said, 'Of course they are, Mr. DeBeckett.'

He smiled. The old man loved children very much. They had been his whole life. The hardest part of his dying was that nothing of his own flesh would be left, no son, no grandchild, no one. He had never married. He would have given almost anything to have a child of his blood with him now – almost anything, except the lurid, grunting price nature exacts, for DeBeckett had never known a woman. His only children were the phantoms of his books . . . and those who came to visit him. He said faintly, 'Let the little sweetlings in.'

The nurse slipped out and the door closed silently behind her. Six children and three adults waited patiently outside, DeBeckett's doctor among them. Quickly she gave him the dimensions of the old man's illness, pulse and temperature, and the readings of the tiny gleaming dials by his pillow as well, though she did not know what they measured. It did not matter. She knew what the doctor was going to say before he said it: 'He can't last another hour. It is astonishing that he lasted this long,' he added, 'but we will have lost something when he goes.'

'He wants you to come in. Especially you —' She glanced around, embarrassed. 'Especially you children.' She had almost said 'little sweetlings' herself, but did not quite dare. Only Elphen DeBeckett could talk like that, even to children. Especially to children. Especially to these children, posed, calm, beautiful, strong and gay. Only the prettiest, sweetest children visited Elphen DeBeckett, half a dozen or a score every day, a year-in, year-out pilgrimage. He would not have noticed if they had been ugly and dull, of course. To DeBeckett all children were sweet, beautiful and bright.

They entered and ranged themselves around the bed, and DeBeckett looked up. The eyes regarded them and a dying voice said, 'Please read to me,' with such resolute sweetness that it frightened. 'From my book,' it added, though they knew well enough what he meant.

The children looked at each other. They ranged from four to eleven, Will, Mike, blonde Celine, brown-eyed Karen, fat Freddy and busy Pat. 'You,' said Pat, who was seven.

'No' said five-year-old Freddy. 'Will.'

'Celine,' said Will. 'Here.'

The girl named Celine took the book from him and began obediently. ' "Coppie thought to herself —" '

'No,' said Pat. 'Open.'

The girl opened the book, embarrassed, glancing at the dying old man. He was smiling at her without amusement, only love. She began to read:

Coppie thought to herself that the geese might be hungry, for she herself ate Lotsandlots. Mumsie often said so, though Coppie had never found out what that mysterious food might be. She could not find any, so took some bread from Brigid Marie Ann-Erica Evangeline, the Cook Whose Name Was So Long That She Couldn't Remember It All Herself. As she walked along Dusty Path to Coppie Brambles's Very Pond—

Celine hesitated, looking at the old man with sharp worry, for he had moaned faintly, like a flower moaning. 'No, love,' he said. 'Go on.' The swelling soft bubble before his heart had turned on him, but he knew he still had time.

The little girl read:

—As she walked along Dusty Path to Coppie Brambles's Very Own Pond, she thought and thought, and what she thought finally came right out of her mouth. It was a Real Gay Think, to be Thought While Charitably Feeding Geese:

They don't make noise like little girls and boys,
And all day long they're aswimming.
They never fret and sputter 'cause they haven't any butter,
They go where the water's wetly brimming.
But say —
Anyway —
I
Like
Geese!

There was more, but the child paused and, after a moment, closed the book. DeBeckett was no longer listening. He was whispering to himself.

On the wall before him was painted a copy of one of the illustrations from the first edition of his book, a delightful picture of Coppie Brambles herself, feeding the geese, admirably showing her shyness and her trace of fear, contrasted with the loutish comedy of the geese. The old man's eyes were fixed on the picture as he whispered. They guessed he was talking to Coppie, the child of eight dressed in the fashions of eighty years ago. They could hardly hear him, but in the silence that fell on the room his voice grew stronger.

He was saying, without joy but without regret, 'No more meadows, no more of the laughter of little children. But I do love them.' He opened his eyes and sat up, waving the nurse away. 'No, my dear,' he said cheerfully, 'it does not matter if I sit up now, you know. Excuse me for my rudeness. Excuse an old and tired man who, for a moment, wished to live on. I have something to say to you all.'

The nurse, catching a sign from the doctor, took up another hypodermic and made it ready. 'Please, Mr. DeBeckett,' she said. Good humored, he permitted her to spray the surface of his wrist with a fine mist of droplets that touched the skin and penetrated it. 'I suppose that is to give me strength,' he said. 'Well, I am grateful for it. I know I must leave you, but there is something I would like to know. I have wondered ... For years I have wondered, but I have not been able to understand the answers when I was told them. I think I have only this one more chance.'

He felt stronger from the fluid that now coursed through his veins, and accepted without fear the price he would have to pay for it. 'As you know,' he said, 'or, I should say, as you children no doubt do not know, some years ago I endowed a research institution, the Coppie Brambles Foundation. I did it for the love of you, you and all of you. Last night I was reading the letter I wrote my attorneys – No. Let us see if you can understand the letter itself; I have it here. Will, can you read?'

Will was nine, freckled darkly on pale skin, red haired and gangling. 'Yes, Mr. DeBeckett.'

'Even hard words,' smiled the dying man.

'Yes, sir.'

DeBeckett gestured at the table beside him, and the boy obediently took up a stiff sheet of paper. 'Please,' said DeBeckett, and the boy began to read in a high-pitched, rapid whine.

' "Children have been all my life and I have not regretted an instant of the years I devoted to their happiness. If I can tell them a little of the wonderful world in which we are, if I can open to them the miracles of life and living, then my joy is unbounded. This I have tried, rather selfishly, to do. I cannot say it was for them! It was for me. For nothing could have given me more pleasure." '

The boy paused.

DeBeckett said gravely, 'I'm afraid this is a Very Big Think, lovelings. Please try to understand. This is the letter I wrote to my attorneys when I instructed them to set up the Foundation. Go on, Will.'

' "But my way of working has been unscientific, I know. I am told that children are not less than we adults, but more. I am told that the grown-up maimers and cheats in the world are only children soiled, that the hagglers of commerce are the infant dreamers whose dreams were denied. I am told that youth is wilder, freer, better than age, which I believe with all my heart, not needing the stories of twenty-year-old mathematicians and infant Mozarts to lay a proof.

' "In the course of my work I have been given great material rewards. I wish that this money be spent for those I love. I have worked with the heart, but perhaps my money can help someone to work with the mind, in this great new science of psychology which I do not understand, in all of the other sciences which I understand even less. I must hire other eyes.

' "I direct, then, that all of my assets other than my books and my homes be converted into cash, and that this money be used to further the study of the child, with the aim of releasing him from the corrupt adult cloak that smothers him, of freeing him for wisdom, tenderness and love." '

'That,' said DeBeckett sadly, 'was forty years ago.'

He started at a sound. Overhead a rocket was clapping through the sky, and DeBeckett looked wildly around. 'It's all right, Mr. DeBeckett,' comforted little Pat. 'It's only a plane.'

He allowed her to soothe him. 'Ah, loveling,' he said. 'And can you answer my question?'

'What it says in the 'Cyclopedia, Mr. DeBeckett?'

'Why – Yes, if you know it, my dear.'

Surprisingly the child said, as if by rote : 'The Institute was founded in 1976 and at once attracted most of the great workers in pediatric analysis, who were able to show Wilt-shanes's Effect in the relationship between glandular and mental development. Within less than ten years a new projective analysis of the growth process permitted a reorientation of basic pedagogy from a null-positive locus. The effects were immediate. The first generation of —'

She stopped, startled. The old man was up on his elbow, his eyes blazing at her in wonder and fright. 'I'm —' She looked around at the other children for help and at once wailed, 'I'm sorry, Mr. DeBeckett!' and began to cry.

The old man fell back, staring at her with a sort of unbelieving panic. The little girl wept abundantly. Slowly DeBeckett's expression relaxed and he managed a sketchy smile.

He said, 'There, sweetest. You startled me. But it was charming of you to memorize all that!'

'I learned it for you,' she sobbed.

'I didn't understand. Don't cry.' Obediently the little girl dried her eyes as DeBeckett stretched out a hand to her.

But the hand dropped back on the quilt. Age, surprise and the drug had allied to overmaster the dwindling resources of Elphen DeBeckett. He wandered to the phantoms on the wall. 'I never understood what they did with my money,' he told Coppie, who smiled at him with a shy, painted smile. 'The children kept coming, but they never said.'

'Poor man,' said Will absently, watching him with a child's uncommitted look.

The nurse's eyes were bright and wet. She reached for the

hypodermic, but the doctor shook his head.

'Wait,' he said, and walked to the bed. He stood on tiptoe to peer into the dying man's face. 'No, no use. Too old. Can't survive organ transplant, certainty of cytic shock. No feasible therapy.' The nurse's eyes were now flowing. The doctor said to her, with patience but not very much patience, 'No alternative. Only kept him going this long from gratitude.'

The nurse sobbed, 'Isn't there *anything* we can do for him?'

'Yes.' The doctor gestured, and the lights on the diagnostic dials winked out. 'We can let him die.'

Little Pat hiked herself up on a chair, much too large for her, and dangled her feet. 'Be nice to get rid of this furniture, anyway,' she said. 'Well, nurse? He's dead. Don't wait.' The nurse looked rebelliously at the doctor, but the doctor only nodded. Sadly the nurse went to the door and admitted the adults who had waited outside. The four of them surrounded the body and bore it gently through the door. Before it closed the nurse looked back and wailed: 'He loved you!'

The children did not appear to notice. After a moment Pat said reflectively, 'Sorry about the book. Should have opened it.'

'He didn't notice,' said Will, wiping his hands. He had touched the old man's fingers.

'No. Hate crying, though.'

The doctor said, 'Nice of you. Helped him, I think.' He picked up the phone and ordered a demolition crew for the house. 'Monument?'

'Oh, yes,' said another child. 'Well. Small one, anyway.'

The doctor, who was nine, said, 'Funny. Without him, what? A few hundred thousand dollars and the Foundation makes a flexible world, no more rigid adults, no more —' He caught himself narrowly. The doctor had observed before that he had a tendency to over-identify with adults, probably because his speciality had been geriatrics. Now that Elphen DeBeckett was dead, he no longer had a speciality.

'Miss him somehow,' said Celine frankly, coming over to look over Will's shoulder at the quaint old murals on the wall. 'What the nurse said, true enough. He loved us.'

'And clearly we loved him,' piped Freddy, methodically sorting through the contents of the dead man's desk. 'Would have terminated him with the others otherwise, wouldn't we?'

Nightmare With Zeppelins

The Zeppelin dirigible balloons bombed London again last night and I got little sleep what with the fire brigade clanging down the street and the anti-aircraft guns banging away. Bad news in the morning post. A plain card from Emmie to let me know that Sam's gone, fast and without much pain. She didn't say, but I suppose it was the 'flu, which makes him at least the fifth of the old lib-lab boys taken off this winter. And why not? We're in our seventies and eighties. It's high time.

Shaw said as much the other day when I met him on the steps of the Museum reading room, he striding in, I doddering out. In that brutal, flippant way of his, he was rather funny about how old Harry Lewes was standing in the way of youngsters like himself, but I can't bring myself to put his remarks down; they would be a little too painful to contemplate.

Well, he's quite recovered from that business with his foot that gave us all such a fright. Barring the 'flu, he may live to my age, and about 1939 bright youngsters now unborn will be watching him like hawks for the smallest sign of rigidity, of eccentricity, and saying complacently: 'Grand old boy, G.B.S. Such a pity he's going the least bit soft upstairs.' And I shall by then be watching from Olympus, and chuckling.

Enough of him. He has the most extraordinary way of getting into everybody's conversation, though it is true that my own conversation does wander, these bad days. I did not think that the second decade of the twentieth century would be like this, though, as I have excellent reason to be, I am glad it is not worse.

I am really quite unhappy and uncomfortable as I sit here at the old desk. Though all the world knows I don't hold with personal service for the young and healthy, I am no longer a member of either of those classes. I do miss the ministrations of Bagley, who at this moment is probably lying in a frozen trench and even more uncomfortable than I. I can't seem to build as warm a fire as he used to. The coals won't go right. Luckily, I know what to do when I am unhappy and uncomfortable: work.

Anyway, Wells is back from France. He has been talking, he says, to some people at the Cavendish Laboratory, wherever that is. He told me we must make a 'radium bomb.' I wanted to ask: 'Must we, Wells? Must we, *really*?'

He says the great virtue of a radium bomb is that it explodes *and keeps on exploding* – for hours, days, weeks. The italics are Wells's – one could hear them in his rather high-pitched voice – and he is welcome to them.

I once saw an explosion which would have interested Wells and, although it did not *keep on exploding*, it was as much of an explosion as I ever care to see.

I thought of telling him so. But, if he believed me, there would be a hue and a cry – I wonder, was I ever once as *consecrated* as he? – and if he did not, he might all the same use it for the subject of one of his 'scientific' romances. After I am gone, of course, but surely that event cannot be long delayed, and in any case that would spoil it. And I want the work. I do not think I have another book remaining – forty-one fat volumes will have to do – but this can hardly be a book.

A short essay; it must be short if it is not to become an autobiography and, though I have resisted few temptations in my life, I mean to fight that one off to the end. That was another jeer of Shaw's. Well, he scored off me, for I confess that some such thought had stirred in my mind.

My lifelong struggle with voice and pen against social injustice had barely begun in 1864, and yet I had played a part in three major work stoppages, published perhaps a dozen pamphlets and was the editor and principal contributor of the still-remembered *Labour's Voice*. I write with what must look like immodesty only to explain how it was that I came to the attention of Miss Carlotta Cox. I was working with the furious energy of a very young man who has discovered his vocation, and no doubt Miss Cox mistook my daemon – now long gone, alas! – for me.

Miss Cox was a member of that considerable group of ruling-class Englishmen and women who devote time, thought and money to improving the lot of the working-man. Everybody knows of good Josiah Wedgewood, Mr. William Morris, Miss Nightingale; they were the great ones. Perhaps I alone today remember Miss Cox, but there were hundreds like her and pray God there will always be.

She was then a spinster in her sixties and had spent most of her life giving away her fortune. She had gone once in her youth to the cotton mills whence that fortune had come, and knew after her first horrified look what her course must be. She instructed her man of business to sell all her shares in that Inferno of sweated labour and for the next forty years, as she always put it, attempted to make restitution.

She summoned me, in short, to her then-celebrated stationer's shop and, between waiting on purchasers of nibs and foolscap, told me her plan. I was to go to Africa.

Across the Atlantic, America was at war within herself. The rebellious South was holding on, not with any hope of subduing the North, but in the expectation of support from England.

England herself was divided. Though England had abolished slavery on her own soil almost a century earlier, still the detestable practise had its apologists, and there were those who held the rude blacks incapable of assuming the dignities of freedom. I was to seek out the Dahomeys and the Congolese on their own grounds and give the lie to those who thought them less than men.

'Tell England,' said Miss Cox, 'that the so-called primitive Negroes possessed great empires when our fathers lived in wattle huts. Tell England that the black lawgivers of Solomon's time are true representatives of their people, and that the monstrous caricature of the plantation black is a venal creation of an ignoble class!'

She spoke like that, but she also handed me a cheque for two hundred and fifty pounds to defray my expenses of travel and to subsidize a wide distribution of the numbers of *Labour's Voice* which would contain my correspondence.

Despite her sometimes grotesque manner, Miss Cox's project was not an unwise one. Whatever enlightenment could be bought at a price of two hundred and fifty pounds was a blow at human slavery. Nor, being barely twenty, was I much distressed by the thought of a voyage to strange lands.

In no time at all, I had turned the direction of *Labour's Voice* over to my tested friends and contributors Mr. Samuel Blackett and Miss Emma Chatto (they married a month later) and in a week I was aboard a French 'composite ship,' iron of frame and wooden of skin, bound for a port on the Dark Continent, the home of mystery and enchantment.

So we thought of it in those days and so, in almost as great degree, do we think of it today, though I venture to suppose that, once this great war is over, those same creations of Count Zeppelin which bombed me last night may dispel some of the mystery, exorcize the enchantment and bring light into the darkness. May it be so, though I trust that whatever discoveries these aeronauts of tomorrow it may bring, will not repeat the discovery Herr Faesch made known to me in 1864.

The squalor of ocean travel in those days is no part of my story. It existed and I endured it for what seemed like an eternity, but at last I bade farewell to *Le Flamant* and all her roaches, rats and stench. Nor does it become this memoir to discuss the tragic failure of the mission Miss Cox had given me.

(Those few who remember my *Peoples of the Earth* will perhaps also remember the account given in the chapter

I entitled 'African Journeyings.' Those, still fewer, whose perception revealed to them an unaccountable gap between the putrid sore throat with which I was afflicted at the headwaters of the Congo and my leave taking on the Gold Coast, will find herewith the chronicle of the missing days.)

It is enough to say that I found no empires in 1864. If they had existed, and I believe they had, they were vanished with Sheba's Queen. I did, however, find Herr Faesch. Or he found me.

How shall I describe Herr Faesch for you? I shan't, Shaw notwithstanding, permit myself so hackneyed a term as 'hardy Swiss;' I am not so far removed from the youthful spring of creation as that. Yet Swiss he was, and surely hardy as well, for he discovered me (or his natives did) a thousand miles from a community of Europeans, deserted by my own bearers, nearer to death than ever I have been since. He told me that I tried thrice to kill him, in my delirium; but he nursed me well and I lived. As you see.

He was a scientific man, a student of Nature's ways, and a healer, though one cure was beyond him. For, sick though I was, he was more ravaged by destructive illness than I. I woke in a firelit hut with a rank poultice at my throat and a naked savage daubing at my brow, and I was terrified; no, not of the native, but of the awful cadaverous face, ghost-white, that frowned down at me from the shadows.

That was my first sight of Herr Faesch.

When, a day later, I became able to sit up and to talk, I found him a gentle and brave man, whose English was every bit as good as my own, whose knowledge surpassed that of any human I met before or since. But the mark of death was on him. In that equatorial jungle, his complexion was alabaster. Ruling the reckless black warriors who served him, his strength yet was less than a child's. In those steaming afternoons when I hardly dared stir from my cot for fear of stroke, he wore gloves and a woollen scarf at his neck.

We had, in all, three days together. As I regained my

health, his health dwindled.

He introduced himself to me as a native of Geneva, that colorful city on the finest lake of the Alps. He listened courteously while I told him of my own errand and did me, and the absent Miss Cox, the courtesy of admiring the spirit which prompted it – though he was not sanguine of my prospects of finding the empires.

He said nothing of what had brought him to this remote wilderness, but I thought I knew. Surely gold. Perhaps diamonds or some other gem, but I thought not; gold was much more plausible.

I had picked up enough of the native dialect to catch perhaps one word in twenty of what he said to his natives and they to him – enough, at any rate, to know that when he left me in their charge for some hours, that first day, he was going to a hole in the ground. It could only be a mine, and what, I asked myself, would a European trouble to mine in the heart of unexplored Africa but gold?

I was wrong, of course. It was not gold at all.

Wells says that they are doing astonishing things at the Cavendish Laboratory, but I do think that Herr Faesch might have astonished even Wells. Certainly he astonished me. On the second day of my convalescence, I found myself strong enough to be up and walking about.

Say that I was prying. Perhaps I was. It was oppressively hot – I dared not venture outside – and yet I was too restless to lie abed waiting for Herr Faesch's return. I found myself examining the objects on his camp table and they were, indeed, nuggets. But the nuggets were not gold. They were a silvery metal, blackened and discolored, but surely without gold's yellow hue; they were rather small, like irregular lark's eggs, and yet they were queerly heavy. Perhaps there was a score of them, aggregating about a pound or two.

I rattled them thoughtfully in my hand, and then observed

that across the tent, in a laboratory jar with a glass stopper, there were perhaps a dozen more – yes, and in yet another place in that tent, in a pottery dish, another clutch of the things. I thought to bring them close together so that I might compare them. I fetched the jar and set it on the table; I went after the pellets in the pottery dish.

Herr Faesch's voice, shaking with emotion, halted me. 'Mr. Lewes!' he whispered harshly. 'Stop, sir!'

I turned, and there was the man, his eyes wide with horror, standing at the flap of the tent. I made my apologies, but he waved them aside.

'No, no,' he croaked, 'I know you meant no harm. But I tell you, Mr. Lewes, you were very near to death a moment ago.'

I glanced at the pellets. 'From these, Herr Faesch?'

'Yes, Mr. Lewes. From those.' He tottered into the tent and retrieved the pottery dish from my hands. Back to its corner it went; then the jar, back across the tent again. 'They must not come together. No, sir,' he said, nodding thoughtfully, though I had said nothing with which he might have been agreeing, 'they must not come together.'

He sat down. 'Mr. Lewes,' he whispered, 'have you ever heard of uranium?' I had not. 'Or of pitchblende? No? Well,' he said earnestly, 'I assure you that you will. These ingots, Mr. Lewes, are uranium, but not the standard metal of commerce. No, sir. They are a rare variant form, indistinguishable by the most delicate of chemical tests from the ordinary metal, but possessed of characteristics which are – I shall merely say "wonderful," Mr. Lewes, for I dare not use the term which comes first to mind.'

'Remarkable,' said I, feeling that some such response was wanted.

He agreed. 'Remarkable indeed, my dear Mr. Lewes! You really cannot imagine how remarkable. Suppose I should tell you that the mere act of placing those few nuggets you discovered in close juxtaposition to each other would liberate an immense amount of energy. Suppose I should tell you that if a certain critical quantity of this metal should be joined together, an explosion would result. Eh, Mr. Lewes? What of that?'

I could only say again, 'Remarkable, Herr Faesch.' I knew nothing else to say. I was not yet one-and-twenty, I had had no interest in making chemists' stinks, and much of what he said was Greek to me – or was science to me, which was worse, for I should have understood the Greek tolerably well. Also a certain apprehension lingered in my mind. That terrible white face, those fired eyes, his agitated speech – I could not be blamed, I think. I believed he might be mad. And though I listened, I heard not, as he went on to tell me of what his discovery might mean.

The next morning he thrust a sheaf of manuscript at me. 'Read, Mr. Lewes!' he commanded me and went off to his mine; but something went wrong. I drowsed through a few pages and made nothing of them except that he thought in some way his nuggets had affected his health. There was a radiant glow in the mine, and the natives believed that glow meant sickness and in time death, and Herr Faesch had come to agree with the natives. A pity, I thought absently, turning in for a nap.

A monstrous smashing sound awakened me. No one was about. I ran out, thrusting aside the tent flap and there, over a hill, through the interstices of the trees, I saw a huge and angry cloud. I don't know how to describe it; I have never since seen its like, and pray God the world never shall again until the end of time.

Five miles away it must have been, but there was heat from it; the tent itself was charred. Tall it was – I don't know how tall, stretching straight and thin from the ground to a toadstool crown shot with lightnings.

The natives came after a time, and though they were desperately afraid, I managed to get from them that it was Herr Faesch's mine that had blown up, along with Herr Faesch and a dozen of themselves. More than that, they would not say.

And I never saw one of them again. In a few days, when I was strong enough, I made my way back to the river and there I was found and helped – I have never known by whom. Half dazed, my fever recurring, I remember only endless journeying, until I found myself near a port.

Yes, there was explosion enough for any man.

That whippersnapper Wells! Suppose, I put it to you, that some such 'radium bomb' should be made. Conceive the captains of Kaiser Will's dirigible fleet possessed of a few nuggets apiece such as those Herr Faesch owned half a century ago. Imagine them cruising above the city of London, sowing their dragon's-teeth pellets in certain predetermined places, until in time a sufficient accumulation was reached to set the whole thing off. Can you think what horror it might set free upon the world.

And so I have never told this story, nor ever would if it were not for those same Zeppelin dirigible balloons. Even now I think it best to withhold it until this war is over, a year or two perhaps. (And that will probably make it posthumous – if only to accommodate Shaw – but no matter.)

I have seen a great deal. I know what I know, and I feel what I feel; and I tell you, this marvelous decade that stretches ahead of us after this present war will open new windows on freedom for the human race. Can it be doubted? Poor Bagley's letters from the trenches tell me that the very *poilus* and Tommies are determined to build a new world on the ruins of the old.

Well, perhaps Herr Faesch's nuggets will help them, these wiser, nobler children of the dawn who are to follow us. They will know what to make of them. One thing is sure: Count Zeppelin has made it impossible for Herr Faesch's metal ever to be used for war. Fighting on the ground itself was terrible enough; this new dimension of warfare will end it. Imagine sending dirigibles across the skies to sow such horrors! Imagine what monstrous brains might plan such an assault! Merciful heaven. They wouldn't dare.

Best Friend

Moray smoothed his whiskers with one hand as he pressed down on the accelerator and swung easily into the top speed lane. Snapping the toggle into a constant eighty-per, he lit a meat-flavored cigarette and replaced the small, darkly warm bar of metal in its socket. He hummed absently to himself. Nothing to do after you were in your right lane – not like flying. He turned on the radio.

'– by Yahnn Bastiën Bock,' said the voice. Moray listened; he didn't know the name.

Then there breathed into the speeding little car the sweetly chilly intervals of a flute-stop. Moray smiled. He liked a simple melody. The music ascended and descended like the fiery speck on an oscillograph field; slowed almost to stopping, and then the melody ended. Why, Moray wondered plaintively, couldn't all music be like that? Simple and clear, without confusing by-play. The melody rose again, with a running mate in the oboe register, and like a ceremonial dance of old days they intertwined and separated, the silvery flute-song and the woody nasal of the oboe. The driver of the little car grew agitated. Suddenly, with a crash, diapasons and clarions burst into the tonal minuet and circled heavily about the principals.

Moray started and snapped off the radio. Try as he would, he never could get used to the Masters' music, and he had never known one of his people who could. He stared out of the window and stroked his whiskers again, forcing his thoughts into less upsetting channels.

A staccato buzz sounded from the dashboard. Moray looked at the road-signs and swung into a lower speed-lane, and then into another. He looped around a ramp intersection and drove into a side-street, pulling up before a huge apartment dwelling.

Moray climbed out into the strip of fuzzy pavement that

extended to the lobby of the building. He had to wait a few moments for one of the elevators to discharge its burden; then he got in and pressed the button that would take him to Floor L, where lived Birch, whom he greatly wanted to marry.

The elevator door curled back and he stepped out into the foyer. He quickly glanced at himself in a long pier glass in the hall, flicked some dust from his jacket. He advanced to the door of Birch's apartment and grinned into the photo-eye until her voice invited him in.

Moray cast a glance about the room as he entered. Birch was nowhere to be seen, so he sat down patiently on a low couch and picked up a magazine. It was lying opened to a story called, 'The Feline Foe.'

'Fantastic,' he muttered. All about an invading planetoid from interstellar space inhabited by cat-people. He felt his skin crawl at the thought, and actually growled deep in his throat. The illustrations were terrifying real – in natural color, printed in three-ply engravings. Each line was a tiny ridge, so that when you moved your head from side to side the figures moved and quivered, simulating life. One was of a female much like Birch, threatened by one of the felines. The caption said, ' "Now," snarled the creature, "we shall see who will be Master!" '

Moray closed the magazine and put it aside. 'Birch!' he called protestingly.

In answer she came through a sliding door and smiled at him. 'Sorry I kept you waiting,' she said.

'That's all right,' said Moray. 'I was looking at this thing.' He held up the magazine.

Birch smiled again. 'Well, happy birthday!' she cried. 'I didn't forget. How does it feel to be thirteen years old?'

'Awful. Joints cracking, hair coming out in patches, and all.' Moray was joking; he had never felt better, and thirteen was the prime of life to his race. 'Birch,' he said suddenly. 'Since I *am* of age, and you and I have been friends for a long time —'

'Not just now, Moray,' she said swiftly. 'We'll miss your

show. Look at the time!'

'All right,' he said, leaning back and allowing her to flip on the telescreen. 'But remember, Birch – I have something to say to you later.' She smiled at him and sat back into the circle of his arm as the screen commenced to flash with color.

The view was of a stage, upon which was an elaborately robed juggler. He bowed and rapidly, to a muttering accompaniment of drums, began to toss discs into the air. Then, when he had a dozen spinning and flashing in the scarlet light, two artists stepped forward and juggled spheres of a contrasting color, and then two more with conventional Indian clubs, and yet two more with open-necked bottles of fluid.

The drums rolled. 'Hup!' shouted the master-juggler, and pandemonium broke loose upon the stage, the artists changing and interchanging, hurling a wild confusion of projectiles at each others' heads, always recovering and keeping the flashing baubles in the air. 'Hup!' shouted the chief again, and as if by magic the projectiles returned to the hands of the jugglers. Balancing them on elbows and heads they bowed precariously, responding to the radioed yelps of applause from the invisible audience.

'They're wonderful!' exclaimed Birch, her soft eyes sparkling.

'Passably good,' agreed Moray, secretly delighted that his suggested entertainment was a success from the start.

Next on the bill was a young male singer, who advanced and bowed with a flutter of soulful eyelids. His song was without words, as was usual among Moray's people. As the incredible headtones rose without breaking, he squirmed ecstatically in his seat, remembering the real pain he had felt earlier in the night, listening to the strange, confusing music of the Masters.

Moray was in ecstasy, but there was a flaw in his ecstasy. Though he was listening with all his soul to the music, yet under the music some little insistent call for attention was coming through. Something very important, not repeated. He tried to brush it aside . . .

Birch nudged him sharply, a little light that you might have called horror in her eyes. 'Moray, your call! Didn't you hear it?'

Moray snatched from a pocket the little receiving set his people always carried with them. Suddenly, and unmuffled this time, shrilled the attention-demanding musical note. Moray leaped up with haste . . .

But he hesitated. He was undecided – incredibly so. 'I don't want to go,' he said slowly to Birch, astonishment at himself in every word.

The horror in Birch's eyes was large now. 'Don't want to! Moray! It's your *Master*!'

'But it isn't – well, fair,' he complained. 'He couldn't have found out that I was with you tonight. Maybe he does know it. And if he had the heart to investigate he would know that – that —' Moray swallowed convulsively. 'That you're more important to me than even he is!' he finished rapidly.

'Don't say that!' she cried, agitated. 'It's like a crime! Moray you'd better go.'

'All right,' he said sullenly, catching up his cape. And he had known all along that he would go. 'You stay here and finish the show. I can get to the roof alone.'

Moray stepped from the apartment into a waiting elevator and shot up to the top of the building. 'I need a fast plane,' he said to an attendant. 'Master's call.' A speed-lined ship was immediately trundled out before him; he got in and the vessel leaped into the air.

One hundred thousand years of forced evolution had done strange things to the canine family. Artificial mutations, rigorous selection, all the tricks and skills of the animal breeder had created a super-dog. Moray was about four feet tall, but no dwarf to his surroundings, for all the world was built to that scale. He stood on his hind legs, for the buried thigh-joint had been extruded by electronic surgery, and his five fingers were long and tapering, with beautifully formed claws capable of the finest artisanry.

And Moray's face was no more canine than your face is simian. All taken in all, he would have been a peculiar but not a fantastic figure could he have walked out into a city of the Twentieth Century. He might easily have been taken for nothing stranger than a dwarf.

Indeed, the hundred thousand years had done more to the Masters than to their dogs. As had been anticipated, the brain had grown and the body shrunk, and there had been a strong tendency toward increased myopia and shrinkage of the distance between the eyes. Of the thousands of sports born to the Masters who had volunteered for genetic experimentation, an indicative minority had been born with a single, unfocussable great eye over a sunken nosebridge, showing a probable future line of development.

The Masters labored no longer; that was for the dog people and more often for the automatic machines. Experimental research, even, was carried on by the companion race, the Masters merely collating the tabulated results, and deducing from and theorizing upon them.

Humankind was visibly growing content with less in every way. The first luxury they had relinquished had been gregariousness. For long generations men had not met for the joy of meeting. There was no such thing as an infringement on the rights of others; a sort of telepathy adjusted all disputes.

Moray's plane roared over the Andes, guided by inflexible directives. A warning sounded in his half-attentive ears; with a start he took over the controls of the craft. Below him, high on the peak of an extinct volcano, he saw the square white block which housed his Master. Despite his resentment at being snatched away from Birch he felt a thrill of excitement at the sensed proximity of his guiding intelligence.

He swung the plane down and grooved it neatly in a landing notch which automatically, as he stepped out, swung round on silent pivots and headed the plane ready for departure.

Moray entered through a door that rolled aside as he approached. His nostrils flared. Almost at the threshold of scent he could feel the emanations of his Master. Moray entered the long, hot corridor that led to his Master's living quarters, and paused before a chrome-steel door.

In a few seconds the door opened, silently, and Moray entered a dark room, his face twitching with an exciting presence. He peered through the gloom, acutely aware of the hot, moist atmosphere of the chamber. And he saw his Master – tiny, shrivelled, quite naked, his bulging skull supported by the high back of the chair.

Moray advanced slowly and stood before the seated human. Without opening his eyes, the Master spoke in a slow, thin voice.

'Moray, this is your birthday.' There was no emphasis on one word more than another; the tone was that of a deaf man.

'Yes, Master,' said Moray. 'A – friend and I were celebrating it when you called. I came as quickly as possible.'

The voice piped out again, 'I have something for you, Moray. A present.' The eyes opened for the first time, and one of the Master's hands gripped spasmodically a sort of lever in his chair. The eyes did not see Moray, they were staring straight ahead; but there was a shallow crease to the ends of his lips that might have been an atavistic muscle's attempt at a smile. A panel swung open in the wall, and there rolled out a broad, flat dolly bearing an ancient and thoroughly rotted chest. Through the cracks in the wood there was seen a yellowish gleam of ancient paper.

The Master continued speaking, though with evidence of a strain. Direct oral conversation told on the clairvoyant, accustomed to the short cuts of telepathy. 'These are the biographies of the lives of the North American Presidents. When you were very young – perhaps you do not remember – you expressed curiosity about them. I made arrangements then to allow you to research the next important find of source-material on the subject. This is it. It was discovered six months ago, and I have saved it for your birthday.'

There was a long silence, and Moray picked up one of the books. It had been treated with preservatives, he noted, and was quite ready for work. He glanced at a title page unenthusiastically. What had interested him in his childhood was boring in full maturity.

'Are you ready to begin now?' whispered the human.

Moray hesitated. The strange confusion that he had felt was growing in him again, wordlessly, like a protesting howl. 'Excuse me, please,' he stammered, stepping back a pace.

The Master bent a look of mild surprise upon him.

'I am sorry. I – I don't wish to do this work.' Moray forced himself to keep his eyes on the Master. There was a quick grimace on the face of the human, who had closed his eyes and was slumped against the back of the chair. His sunken chin twitched and fell open.

The Master did not answer Moray for a long minute. Then his eyes flicked open, he sat erect again, and he said, 'Leave me.'

And then he stared off into space and took no further notice of Moray.

'Please,' said Moray hastily. 'Don't misunderstand, I want very much to read those books. I have wanted to all my life. But I —' He stopped talking. Very obviously, the Master had eliminated Moray from his mind. Just as Moray himself, having had a cinder in his eyes, would drop from his mind the memory of the brief pain.

Moray turned and walked through the door. 'Please,' he repeated softly to himself, then growled in disgust. As he stepped into the plane once more he blinked rapidly. In the hundred thousand years of evolution dogs had learned to weep.

Moray, looking ill, slumped deeper into the pneumatic couch's depths. Birch looked at him with concern in her warm eyes. 'Moray,' she said worriedly, 'when did you sleep last?'

'It doesn't matter,' he said emptily. 'I've been seeing the town.'

'Can I give you something to eat?'

'No,' said Moray. With a trace of guilt he took a little bottle from his pocket and gulped down a couple of white pills. 'I'm not hungry. And this is more fun.'

'It's up to you,' she said. There was a long silence, and Moray picked up sheets of paper that were lying on a table at his elbow. 'Assignments as of Wednesday,' he read, and then put down the sheaf, rubbing his eyes with a tired motion. 'Are you doing any work now?' he asked.

Birch smiled happily. 'Oh, yes,' she said. 'My Master wants some statistics collated. All about concrete pouring. It's very important work, and I finished it a week ahead of time.'

Moray hesitated, then, as though he didn't care, asked: 'How are you and your Master getting along?'

'Very well indeed. She called me yesterday to see if I needed an extension of time for the collation. She was very pleased to find I'd finished it already.'

'You're lucky,' said Moray shortly. And inside himself, bursting with grief, he wondered what was wrong between his own Master and himself. Three weeks; not a single call. It was dreadful. 'Oh, Birch, I think I'm going mad!' he cried.

He saw that she was about to try to soothe him. 'Don't interrupt,' he said. 'The last time I saw my Master I – made him unhappy. I was sure he would want me again in a few days, but he seems to have abandoned me completely. Birch, does that ever happen?'

She looked frightened. The thought was appalling. 'Maybe,' she said hastily. 'I don't know. But he wouldn't do that to you, Moray. You're too clever. Why, he needs you just as much as you need him!'

Moray sighed and stared blankly. 'I wish I could believe that.' He took out the little pill-bottle again, but Birch laid a hand on his.

'Don't take any more, please, Moray,' she whispered, trying desperately to ease his sorrow. 'Moray – a while ago you wanted to ask me something. Will you ask me now?'

'I wanted to ask you to marry me – is that what you mean?'

'Yes. To both questions, Moray. I will.'

He laughed harshly. 'Me! How can you marry me? For all I know I've lost my Master. If I have, I – I'm no longer a person. You don't know what it's like, Birch, losing half your mind, and your will, and all the ambition you ever had. I'm no good now, Birch.' He rose suddenly and paced up and down the floor. 'You *can't* marry me!' he burst out. 'I think I'll be insane within a week! I'm going now. Maybe you'd better forget you ever knew me.' He slammed out of the room and raced down the stairs, not waiting for an elevator.

The street-lights were out; it was the hour before dawn. Obeying a vagrant impulse, he boarded a moving strip of sidewalk and was carried slowly out to one of the suburbs of the metropolis. At the end of the line, where the strip turned back on itself and began the long journey back to Central Square, he got off and walked into the half-cultivated land.

He had often wondered – fearfully – of the fate of those of his people who had been abandoned by their Masters. Where did they go? Into the outlands, as he was?

He stared at the darkness of the trees and shrubs, suddenly realizing that he had never known the dark before. Wherever his people had gone there had been light – light in the streets, light in their cars and planes, light even at night when they slept.

He felt the hair on his head prickle and rise. How did one go wild? he wondered confusedly. Took off their clothes, he supposed.

He felt in his pockets and drew out, one by one, the symbols of civilization. A few slot-machine tokens, with which one got the little white pills. Jingling keys to his home, office, car, locker, and closet. Wallet of flexible steel, containing all his personal records. A full bottle of the pills – and another, nearly empty.

Mechanically he swallowed two tablets of the drug and

threw the bottle away. A little plastic case ... and as he stared at it, a diamond-hard lump in his throat, a fine, thin whistle shrilled from its depths.

Master's call! He was wanted!

Moray climbed from the plane under the frowning Andes and almost floated into the corridor of his Master's dwelling. The oppressive heat smote him in the face, but he was near laughing for joy when he opened the door and saw his Master sitting naked in the gloom.

'You are slow, Moray,' said the Master, without inflection.

Moray experienced a sudden chill. He had not expected this. Confusedly he had pictured a warm reconciliation, but there was no mistaking the tone of the Master's voice. Moray felt very tired and discouraged. 'Yes,' he said. 'You called me when I was out at the fields.'

The Master did not frown, nor did he smile. Moray knew these moods of the cold, bleak intellect that gave him the greater part of his own intelligence and personality. Yet there was no greater tragedy in the world of his people than to be deserted – or, rather, to lose rapport with this intelligence. It was not insanity, and yet it was worse.

'Moray,' said the Master, 'you are a most competent laboratory technician. And you have an ability for archaeology. You are assigned to a task which involves both these divisions. I wish you to investigate the researches of Carter Hawkes, time, about the Fifteenth Century Anno Cubriensis. Determine his conclusions and develop, on them, a complete solution to what he attempted to resolve.'

'Yes,' said Moray dully. Normally he would have been elated at the thought that he had been chosen, and he consciously realized that it was his duty to be elated, but the chilly voice of his conscience told him that this was no affectionate assignment, but merely the use of a capable tool.

'What is the purpose of this research?' he asked formally,

his voice husky with fatigue and indulgence in the stimulant drug.

'It is of great importance. The researches of Hawkes, as you know, were concerned with explosives. It was his barbarous intention to develop an explosive of such potency that one charge would be capable of destroying an enemy nation. Hawkes, of course, died before his ambition was realized, but we have historical evidence that he was on the right track.'

'Chief among which,' interrupted Moray – deferentially – 'is the manner of his death.'

There was no approval in the Master's voice as he answered, 'You know of the explosion in which he perished. Now, at this moment, the world is faced with a crisis more terrible than any ancient war could have been. It involves a shifting of the continental blocks of North America. The world now needs the Hawkes explosive, to provide the power for re-stabilizing the continent. All evidence has been assembled for your examination in the workroom. Speed is essential if catastrophe is to be averted.'

Moray was appalled. The fate of a continent in his hands! 'I shall do my best,' he said nervelessly, and walked from the room.

Moray straightened his aching body and turned on the lights. He set the last of a string of symbols down on paper and leaned back to stare at them. The formula – complete!

Moray was convinced that he had the right answer, through the lightning-like short cuts of reasoning, which humans called 'canine intuition.' Moray might have felt pride in that ability – but, he realized, it was a mirage. The consecutivity of thought of the Masters – not Moray nor any of his people could really concentrate on a single line of reasoning for more than a few seconds. In the synthesis of thought Moray's people were superb. In its analysis ...

A check-up on the formula was essential. Repeating the

formula aloud, Moray's hands grasped half a dozen ingredients from the shelves of the lab, and precisely compounded them in the field of a micro-inspection device. Actually, Moray was dealing with units measured in single molecules, and yet his touch was as sure as though he were handling beakers-full.

Finally titrated, the infinitesimal compound was set over a cherry-red electric grid to complete its chain of reactions and dry. Then it would explode, Moray realized – assuming he had the formula correct. But, with such a tiny quantity, what would be the difference?

Perhaps – at utmost – the room would be wrecked. But there was no time to take the stuff to the firing-chambers that were suspended high over the crater of the extinct volcano on flexible steel masts, bent and supported to handle almost any shock.

Moray swallowed two more pellets of the drug. He had to wait for its effect upon him, now, but he dared not take a larger dose.

He strode from the room, putting the formula in his pocket.

Wandering aimlessly through the building, he was suddenly assailed by the hot, wet aura of his Master. He paused, then nudged the door open a trifle and peered longingly within.

The Master was engaged in solitary clairvoyance, his head sagging down on his scrawny chest, veins and muscles visibly pulsing. Even in the utter darkness of his room, he was visible by a thin blue light that exuded from the points and projections of his body to flow about the entire skin.

The Master was utterly unconscious of the presence of his servant. Though Moray was not a child or a fool, he stemmed directly from the beautiful, intelligent creatures that used to hunt and play with men, and he could not stand up to the fierce tide of intellect that flowed in that room. With a smothered sound he turned, about to leave.

Then Moray heard a noise – quiet and almost restful at first, like a swarm of bees passing overhead. And then it rumbled

into a mighty crash that made the elastic construction of the
Master's house quiver as though stricken.

Suddenly he realized – the Hawkes explosive! It had
worked! He looked at his Master, to see the blue glare fade as
though it were being reabsorbed into his body. As the last of it
vanished, lights glowed on around the room, bringing it to its
accustomed shadowy twilight. The Master's head lifted.

'Moray,' he whispered tensely. 'Was that the explosive?'

A thin little ripple of delight surged along Moray's spine.
They could both be blown to splintered atoms in the explosion, and the continent they were trying to save along with
them – he didn't care! His Master had spoken to him!

He knew what he had to do. With a little growl that was
meant to say, 'Pardon!' he raced to the Master's side, picked
him up and flung him over a shoulder – gently. They had to
get out of the building, for it might yet topple on them.

Moray tottered to the door, bent under the double burden;
pushed it open and stepped into the corridor. The Master
couldn't walk, so Moray had to walk for him. They made slow
progress along the interminable hall, but finally they were in
the open. Moray set his burden down, the gangling head swaying, and —

Felt unutterably, incontrovertibly idiotic! For the air was
still and placid; and the building stood firm as a rock; and the
only mark of the Hawkes explosive was a gaping mouth of a
pit where the laboratory had been. Idiot! Not to have remembered that the Hawkes would expend its force *downward*!

Moray peered shamefacedly at his Master. Yet there was
some consolation for him, because there was the skeleton of a
smile on the Master's face. Clearly he had understood Moray's
motives, and ... perhaps Moray's life need not finally be
blighted.

For a long second they stood there looking into each other's
eyes. Then the Master said, gently, 'Carry me to the plane.'

Not stopping to ask why, Moray picked him up once more

and strode buoyantly to the waiting ship. Letting the Master down gently at the plane's door, he helped him in, got in himself, and took his place at the controls.

'Where shall we go?' he ask.

The Master smiled that ghost of a smile again, but Moray could detect a faint apprehension in his expression, too. 'Up, Moray,' he whispered. 'Straight up. You see, Moray, these mountains are volcanic. And they're not quite extinct. We must go away now, up into the air.'

Moray's reflexes were faster than an electron-stream as he whipped around to the knobs and levers that sent the little ship tearing up into the atmosphere. A mile and a half in the sky, he flipped the bar that caused the ship to hover, turned to regard the scene below.

The Master had been right! The explosion had pinked the volcano, and the volcano was erupting in retaliation – a hot curl of lava was snaking into the atmosphere now, seemingly a pseudo-pod reaching to bring them down. But it was thrown up only a few hundred feet; then the lava flow stopped; cataclysmic thunderings were heard and vast boulders were hurled into the sky. It was lucky they'd got away, thought Moray as he watched the ground beneath quiver and shake; and luckier that no other person had been around, for the ship could carry but two.

And as he stared, fascinated, at the turmoil below, he felt a light, soft touch on his arm. It was the Master! – the first time in all Moray's life when the Master had touched him to draw attention, Moray suddenly knew, and rejoiced – he had found his Master again!

'Let us go on, Moray,' whispered the Master. 'We have found that the explosive will work. Our job, just now, is done.'

And as Moray worked the controls that hurled the ship ahead, toward a new home for his Master and toward Birch for himself, he knew that the wings of the ship were of no value at all. Tear them off! he thought, and throw them away! His heart was light enough to bear a world!

The world of Myrion Flowers, which was the world of the
American Negro, was something like an idealized England and
something like the real Renaissance. As it is in some versions
of England, all the members of the upper class were at least
friends of friends. Any Harlem businessman knew automatically who was the new top dog in the music department of
Howard University a week after an upheaval of the faculty.
And as it was in the Florence of Cellini, there was room for
versatile men. An American Negro could be a doctor-builder-
educator-realist-politician. Myrion Flowers was. Boston-born
in 1913 to a lawyer-realist-politician father and a glamorous
show-biz mother, he worked hard, drew the lucky number and
was permitted to enter the schools which led to an M.D. and a
license to practise in the State of New York. Power vacuums
occurred around him during the years that followed, and willy-
nilly he filled them. A construction firm going to waste, needing a little capital and a little common sense – what could he
do? He did it, and accepted its stock. The school board coming to him as a sound man to represent 'ah, your people'? He
was a sound man. He served the board well. A trifling examination to pass for a real-estate license – trifling to him who
had memorized a dozen textbooks in pathology, histology,
anatomy and materia medica – why not? And if they would
deem it such a favor if he spoke for the Fusion candidate, why
should he not speak, and if they should later invite him to
submit names to fill one dozen minor patronage jobs, why
should he not give them the names of the needy persons he
knew?

Flowers was a cold, controlled man. He never married. In
lieu of children he had protégés. These began as Negro
kids from orphanages or hopelessly destitute families; he
backed them through college and postgraduate schools as long

as they worked to the limit of what he considered their abilities; at the first sign of a let-down he axed them. The mortality rate over the years was only about one non-graduate in four – Myrion Flowers was a better predictor of success than any college admissions committee. His successes numbered forty-two when one of them came to him with a brand-new Ph.D. in clinical psychology and made a request.

The protégé's name was Ensal Brubacker. He took his place after dinner in the parlor of Dr. Flowers's Brooklyn brownstone house along with many other suppliants. There was the old woman who wanted an extension of her mortgage and would get it; there was the overstocked appliance dealer who wanted to be bailed out and would not be; there was the mother whose boy had a habit and the husband whose wife was acting stranger and stranger every day; there was the landlord hounded by the building department; there was the cop who wanted a transfer; there was the candidate for the bar who wanted a powerful name as a reference; there was a store-front archbishop who wanted only to find out whether Dr. Flowers was right with God.

Brubacker was admitted to the doctor's study at 9:30. It was only the sixth time he had seen the man who had picked him from an orphanage and laid out some twenty thousand dollars for him since. He found him more withered, colder and quicker than ever.

The doctor did not congratulate him. He said, 'You've got your degree, Brubacker. If you've come to me for advice, I'd suggest that you avoid the academic life, especially in the Negro schools. I know what you should do. You may get nowhere, but I would like to see you try one of the Four-A advertising and public relations firms, with a view to becoming a motivational research man. It's time one Negro was working in the higher levels of Madison Avenue, I believe.'

Brubacker listened respectfully, and when it was time for him to reply he said: 'Dr. Flowers, I'm very grateful of course for everything you've done. I sincerely wish I could – Dr.

Flowers, I want to do research. I sent you my dissertation, but that's only the beginning —'

Myrion Flowers turned to the right filing card in his mind and said icily, 'The Correlation of Toposcopic Displays, Beta-Wave Amplitudes and Perception of Musical Chord Progressions in 1,107 Unselected Adolescents. Very well. You now have your sandwich board with "P", "H" and "D" painted on it, fore and aft. I expect that you will now proceed to the job for which you have been trained.'

'Yes, sir. I'd like to show you a —'

'I do not,' said Dr. Flowers, 'want you to be a beloved old George Washington Carver humbly bending over his reports and test tubes. Academic research is of no immediate importance.'

'No, sir. I —'

'The power centers of America,' said Dr. Flowers, 'are government, where our friend Mr. Wilkins is ably operating, and the executive levels of the large corporations, where I am attempting to achieve what is necessary. I want you to be an executive in a large corporation, Brubacker. You have been trained for that purpose. It is now perhaps barely possible for you to obtain a foothold. It is inconceivable to me that you will not make the effort, neither for me nor for your people.'

Brubacker looked at him in misery, and at last put his face into his hands. His shoulders shook.

Dr. Flowers said scornfully: 'I take it you are declining to make that effort. Good-bye, Brubacker. I do not want to see you again.'

The young man stumbled from the room, carrying a large pig-skin valise which he had not been permitted to open.

As he had expected to overwhelm his benefactor with what he had accomplished he had made no plans for this situation. He could think only of returning to the university he had just left where, perhaps, before his little money ran out, he might obtain a grant. There was not really much hope of that. He had filed no proposals and sought no advice.

It did not help his mood when the overnight coach to Chicago was filling up in Grand Central. He was among the first and took a window seat. Thereafter the empty place beside him was spotted gladly by luggage-burdened matrons, Ivy-League-clad youngsters, harrumphing paper-box salesmen – gladly spotted – and then uncomfortably skimmed past when they discovered that to occupy it they would have to sit next to the   gorilla-rapist-illiterate-tap-dancer-mugger-menace   who happened to be Dr. Ensal Brubacker.

But he was spared loneliness at the very last. The fellow who did drop delightedly into the seat beside him as the train began to move was One of His Own Kind. That is, he was unwashed, unlettered, a quarter drunk on liquor that had never known a tax stamp, and agonizingly high-spirited. He spoke such pure Harlem jive that Brubacker could not understand one word in twenty.

But politeness and a terror of appearing rude forced Brubacker to accept, at 125th Street, a choking swallow from the flat half-pint bottle his seatmate carried. And both of these things, plus an unsupportable sense of something lost, caused him to accept his seatmate's later offer of more paralyzing pleasures. In ten months Brubacker was dead, in Lexington, Kentucky, of pneumonia incurred while kicking the heroin habit, leaving behind him a badly puzzled staff doctor. 'They'll say everything in withdrawal,' he confided to his wife, 'but I wonder how this one ever heard the word "cryptesthesia."'

It was about a month after that that Myrion Flowers received the package containing Brubacker's effects. There had been no one else to send them to.

He was shaken, that controlled man. He had seen many folkgods of his people go the same route, but they were fighters, entertainers or revivalists; he had not expected it of a young, brilliant university graduate. For that reason he did not immediately throw the junk away, but mused over it for some minutes. His next visitor found him with a silvery-coppery sort of helmet in his hands.

Flower's next visitor was a former Corporation Counsel to the City of New York. By attending Dr. Powell's church and having Dr. Flowers take care of his health he kept a well-placed foot in both the principal political camps of the city. He no longer much needed political support, but Flowers had pulled him through one coronary and he was too old to change doctors. 'What have you got there, Myrion?' he asked.

Flowers looked up and said precisely, 'If I can believe the notes of the man who made it, it is a receiver and amplifier for betawave oscillations.'

The Corporation Counsel groaned, 'God preserve me from the medical mind. What's that in English?' But he was surprised to see the expression of wondering awe that came over Flowers's withered face.

'It reads thoughts,' Flowers whispered.

The Corporation Counsel at once clutched his chest, but found no pain. He complained testily, 'You're joking.'

'I don't think I am, Wilmot. The man who constructed this device had all the appropriate dignities – summa cum laude, Dean's List, interviewed by mail by nearly thirty prospective employers. Before they found out the color of his skin, of course. No,' he said reflectively, 'I don't think I'm joking, but there's one way to find out.'

He lifted the helmet towards his head. The Corporation counsel cried out, 'Damn you, Myrion, don't do that!'

Flowers paused. 'Are you afraid I'll read your mind and learn your secrets?'

'At my time of life? When you're my doctor? No, Myrion, but you ought to know I have a bad heart. I don't want you electrocuted in front of my eyes. Besides, what the devil does a Negro want with a machine that will tell him what people are thinking? Isn't guessing bad enough for you?'

Myrion Flowers chose to ignore the latter part of what his

patient had said. 'I don't expect it to electrocute me, and I don't expect this will affect your heart, Wilmot. In any event, I don't propose to be wondering about this thing for any length of time. I don't want to try it when I'm alone and there's no one else here.' He plopped the steel bowl on his head. It fitted badly and was very heavy. An extension cord hung from it, and without pausing Flowers plugged it into a wall socket by his chair.

The helmet whined faintly and Flowers leaped to his feet. He screamed.

The Corporation Counsel moved rapidly enough to make himself gasp. He snatched the helmet from Flowers's head, caught him by the shoulders and lowered him into his chair again. 'You all right?' he growled.

Flowers shuddered epileptically and then controlled himself. 'Thank you, Wilmot. I hope you haven't damaged Dr. Brubacker's device.' And then suddenly, 'It hit me all at once. It *hurt*!'

He breathed sharply and sat up.

From one of his desk drawers he took a physicians' sample bottle of pills and swallowed one without water. 'Everyone was screaming at once,' he said. He started to replace the pills, then saw the Corporation Counsel holding his chest and mutely offered him one.

Then he seemed startled.

He looked into his visitor's eyes. 'I can still hear you.'

'What?'

'It's false angina, I think. But take the pill. But—' he passed a hand over his eyes – 'You thought I was electrocuted, and you wondered how to straighten out my last bill. It's a fair bill, Wilmot. I didn't overcharge you.' Flowers opened his eyes very wide and said, 'The newsboy on the corner cheated me out of my change. He —' swallowed and said, 'The cops in the squad car just turning off Fulton Street don't like my having white patients. One of them is thinking about running in a girl that came here.' He sobbed, 'It didn't stop, Wilmot.'

'For Christ's sake, Myrion, lie down.'

'*It didn't stop.* It's not like a radio. You can't turn it off. Now I can hear – everybody! Every mind for miles around is *pouring into my head* WHAT IT THINKS ABOUT ME – ABOUT ME – ABOUT US!'

Ensal Brubacker, who had been a clinical psychologist and not a radio engineer, had not intended his helmet to endure the strain of continuous operation nor had he thought to provide circuit-breakers. It had been meant to operate for a few moments at most, enough to reroute a few neutrons, open a blocked path or two. One of its parts overheated. Another took too much load as a result, and in a moment the thing was afire. It blew the fuses and the room was in darkness. The elderly ex-Corporation Counsel managed to get the fire out, and then picked up the phone. Shouting to be heard over the screaming of Myrion Flowers, he summoned a Kings County ambulance. They knew Flowers's name. The ambulance was there in nine minutes.

Flowers died some weeks later in the hospital – not Kings County, but he did not know the difference. He had been under massive sedation for almost a month until it became a physiological necessity to taper him off; and as soon as he was alert enough to do so he contrived to hang himself in his room.

His funeral was a state occasion. The crowds were enormous and there was much weeping. The Corporation Counsel was one of those permitted to cast a clod of earth upon the bronze casket, but he did not weep.

No one had ever figured out what the destroyed instrument was supposed to have been, and Wilmot did not tell. There are inventions and inventions, he thought, and reading minds is a job for white men. If even for white men. In the world of Myrion Flowers many seeds might sturdily grow, but some ripe fruits would mature into poison.

No doubt the machine might have broken any mind, listening in on every thought that concerned one. It was maddening and dizzying, and the man who wore the helmet would be harmed in any world; but only in the world of Myrion Flowers would he be hated to death.

Trouble In Time

To begin at the beginning everybody knows that scientists are crazy. I may be either mistaken or prejudiced, but this seems especially true of mathematico-physicists. In a small town like Colchester gossip spreads fast and furiously, and one evening the word was passed around that an outstanding example of the species Doctissimus Dementiae had finally lodged himself in the old frame house beyond the dog-pound on Court Street, mysterious crates and things having been unloaded there for weeks previously.

Abigail O'Liffey, a typical specimen of the low type that a fine girl like me is forced to consort with in a small town, said she had seen the Scientist. 'He had broad shoulders,' she said dreamily, 'and red hair, and a scraggly little moustache that wiggled up and down when he chewed gum.'

'What would you expect it to do?'

She looked at me dumbly. 'He was wearing a kind of garden coat,' she said. 'It was like a painter's, only it was all burned in places instead of having paint on it. I'll bet he discovers things like Paul Pasteur.'

'*Louis* Pasteur,' I said. 'Do you know *his* name, by any chance?'

'Whose – the Scientist's? Clarissa said one of the expressmen told her husband it was Cramer or something.'

'Never heard of him,' I said. 'Good night.' And I slammed the screen door. Cramer, I thought – it was the echo of a name I knew, and a big name at that. I was angry with Clarissa for not getting the name more accurately, and with Abigail for bothering me about it, and most of all with the Scientist for stirring me out of my drowsy existence with remembrances of livelier and brighter things not long past.

So I slung on a coat and sneaked out the back door to get a look at the mystery man, or at least his house. I slunk past the dog-pound, and the house sprang into sight like a Christmas tree – every socket in the place must have been in use, to judge from the flood of light that poured from all windows. There was a dark figure on the unkempt lawn; when I was about ten yards from it and on the verge of turning back it shouted at me: 'Hey, you! Can you give me a hand?'

I approached warily; the figure was wrestling with a crate four feet high and square. 'Sure,' I said.

The figure straightened. 'Oh, so he's a she,' it said. 'Sorry, lady. I'll get a hand truck from inside.'

'Don't bother,' I assured it. 'I'm glad to help.' And I took one of the canvas slings as it took the other, and we carried the crate in, swaying perilously. 'Set it here, please,' he said, dropping his side of the crate. It *was* a he, I saw in the numerous electric bulbs' light, and from all appearances the Scientist Cramer, or whatever his name was.

I looked about the big front parlor, bare of furniture but jammed with boxes and piles of machinery. 'That was the last piece,' he said amiably, noting my gaze. 'Thank you. Can I offer you a scientist's drink?'

'Not – ethyl?' I cried rapturously.

'The same,' he assured me, vigorously attacking a crate that tinkled internally. 'How do you know?'

'Past experience. My Alma Mater was the Housatonic University, School of Chemical Engineering.'

He had torn away the front of the crate, laying bare a neat array of bottles. 'What's a C.E. doing in this stale little place?' he asked, selecting flasks and measures.

'Sometimes she wonders,' I said bitterly. 'Mix me an Ethyl Martini, will you?'

'Sure, if you like them. I don't go much for the fancy swigs myself. Correct me if I'm wrong.' He took the bottle labeled C_2H_5OH. 'Three cubic centimeters?'

'No – you don't start with the ethyl!' I cried. 'Put four minims of fusel oil in a beaker.' He complied. 'Right – now a tenth of a grain of saccharine saturated in theine barbiturate ten per cent solution.' His hands flew through the pharmaceutical ritual. 'And *now* pour in the ethyl slowly, and stir, don't shake.'

He held the beaker to the light. 'Want some color in that?' he asked, immersing it momentarily in liquid air from a double thermos.

'No,' I said. 'What are you having?'

'A simple fusel highball,' he said, expertly pouring and chilling a beakerful, and brightening it with a drop of a purple dye that transformed the colorless drink into a sparkling beverage. We touched beakers and drank deep.

'That,' I said gratefully when I had finished coughing, 'is the first real drink I've had since graduating three years ago. The stuff has a nostalgic appeal for me.'

He looked blank. 'It occurs to me,' he said, 'that I ought to introduce myself. I am Stephen Trainer, late of Mellon, late of Northwestern, late of Cambridge, sometime fellow of the Sidney School of Technology. Now you tell me who you are and we'll be almost even.'

I collected my senses and announced, 'Miss Mabel Evans, late in practically every respect.'

'I am pleased to make your acquaintance, Miss Evans,' he said. 'Won't you sit down?'

'Thank you,' I murmured. I was about to settle on one of the big wooden boxes when he cried out at me.

'For God's sake – not there!'

'And why not?' I asked, moving to another. 'Is that your reserve stock of organic bases?'

'No,' he said. 'That's part of my time machine.'

I looked at him. 'Just a nut, huh?' I said pityingly. 'Just another sometimes capable fellow gone wrong. He thinks he knows what he's doing, and he even had me fooled for a time, but the *idée fixe* has come out at last, and we see the man for what he is – mad as a hatter. Nothing but a time-traveller at the bottom of that mass of flesh and bone.' I felt sorry for him, in a way.

His face grew as purple as the drink in his hand. As though he too had formed the association, he drained it and set it down. 'Listen,' he said. 'I only know one style of reasoning that parallels yours in its scope and utter disregard of logic. Were you ever so unfortunate as to be associated with that miserable charlatan, Dr. George B. Hopper?'

'My physics professor at Housatonic,' I said, 'and whaddya make of that?'

'I am glad of the chance of talking to you,' he said in a voice suddenly hoarse. 'It's no exaggeration to say that for the greater part of my life I've wanted to come across a pupil of Professor Hopper. I've sat under him and over him on various faculties; we even went to Cambridge together – it disgusted both of us. And now at last I have the chance, and now you are going to learn the *truth* about physics.'

'Go on with your lecture,' I muttered skeptically.

He looked at me glassily. 'I *am* going on with my lecture,' he said. 'Listen closely. Take a circle. What is a circle?'

'You tell me,' I said.

'A circle is a closed arc. A circle is composed of an infinite number of straight lines, each with a length of zero, each at an angle infinitesmally small to its adjacent straight lines.'

'I should be the last to dispute the point,' I said judiciously. He reached for the decanter and missed. He reached again grimly, his fist opening and closing, and finally snapping shut on its neck. 'Will you join me once more?' he asked graciously.

'Granted,' I said absently, wondering what was going around in my head.

'*Now* – one point which we must get quite clear in the beginning is that all circles are composed of an in —'

'You said that already,' I interrupted.

'Did I?' he asked with a delighted smile. 'I'm brighter than I thought.' He waggled his head fuzzily. 'Then do you further admit that, by a crude Euclidean axiom which I forget at the moment, all circles are equal?'

'Could be – but so help me, if —' I broke off abruptly as I

realized that I was lying full length on the floor. I shuddered at the very thought of what my aunt would say to *that*.

'The point I was about to make,' he continued without a quaver, 'was that if all circles are *equal*, all circles can be traversed at the same expenditure of effort, money, or what have you.' He stopped and gasped at me, collecting his thoughts. 'All circles can be traversed, also, with the same amount of *time*! No matter whether the circle be the equator or the head of a pin! Now do you see?'

'With the clarity appalling. And the time travelling . . .?'

'Ah – er – yes. The time travelling. Let me think for a moment.' He indicated thought by a Homeric configuration of his eyebrows, forehead, cheeks and chin. 'Do you know,' he finally said with a weak laugh, 'I'm afraid I've forgotten the connection. But my premise is right, isn't it? If it takes the same time to traverse any two circles, and one of them is the universe, and the other is my time wheel—' His voice died under my baleful stare.

'I question your premise vaguely,' I said. 'There's nothing I can exactly put my finger on, but I *believe* it's not quite dry behind the ears.'

'Look,' he said. 'You can question it as much as you like, but it *works*. I'll show you the gimmicks.'

We clambered to our feet. 'There,' he pointed to the box I had nearly sat upon, 'there lies the key to the ages.' And he took up a crowbar and jimmied the top off the crate.

I lifted out carefully the most miscellaneous collection of junk ever seen outside a museum of modern art. 'What, for example,' I asked, gingerly dangling a canvas affair at arms' length, 'does this thing do?'

'One wears it as a belt,' he said. I put the thing on and found that it resolved itself into a normal Sam Browne belt with all sorts of oddments of things dangling from it.

'Now,' he said, 'I have but to plug this into a wall socket, and then, providing you get on the time wheel, out you go like a light – *pouf*!'

'Don't be silly,' I said. 'I'm practically out now in the first place, in the second place I don't care whether I go out *pouf* or *splash* – though the latter is more customary – and in the third place I don't believe your silly old machine works anyway. I dare you to make me go *pouf* – I just dare you!'

'All right,' he said mildly. 'Over there is the time wheel. Get on it.'

The time wheel reminded me of a small hand-turned merry-go-round. I got on it with a good will, and he made it turn. Then he plugged in the lead to a wall socket, and I went out like a light – *pouf*!

There are few things more sobering than time-travel. On going *pouf* I closed my eyes, as was natural. Possibly I screamed a little, too. All I know is when I opened my eyes they were bleary and aching, and certainly nowhere very near the old house past the dog-pound on Court Street. The locale appeared to be something like Rockefeller Center, only without fountains.

I was standing on polished stones – beautifully polished stones which seemed to set the keynote of the surroundings. Everything was beautiful and everything was polished. Before me was a tall, tall building. It was a dark night, and there seemed to be a great lack of illumination in this World of Tomorrow.

I followed my nose into the building. The revolving door revolved without much complaint, and did me the favor of turning on the lights of the lobby.

There were no people there; there were no people anywhere in sight. I tried to shout, and the ghastly echo from the still darkened sections made me tremble to my boots. I didn't try again, but very mousily looked about for an elevator or something. The something turned out to be a button in a vast column, labeled in plain English, 'Slavies' ring.'

I rang, assuring myself that doing so was no confession of inferiority, but merely the seizing of an offered opportunity.

All the lobby lights went out, then, but the column was glowing like mother-of-pearl before a candle. A sort of door opened, and I walked through. 'Why not?' I asked myself grimly.

I seemed to be standing on a revolving staircase – but one that actually revolved! It carried me up like a gigantic corkscrew at a speed that was difficult to determine. It stopped after a few minutes, and another door opened. I stepped through and said 'Thank you' nicely to the goblins of the staircase, and shuddered again as the door slammed murderously fast and hard.

Lights go again at my landing place – I was getting a bit more familiar with this ridiculous civilization. Was everybody away at Bermuda for the summer? I wondered. Then I chattered my teeth.

Corpses! Hundreds of them! I had had the bad taste, I decided, to land in the necropolis of the World of Tomorrow.

On slabs of stone they lay in double rows, great lines of them stretching into the distance of the huge chamber into which I had blundered. Morbid curiosity moved me closer to the nearest stiff. I had taken a course in embalming to get my C.E., and I pondered on the advances of that art.

Something hideously like a bed-lamp clicked on as I bent over the mummified creature. Go above! With a rustling like the pages of an ancient book it moved – flung its arm over its eyes!

I'm afraid I may have screamed. But almost immediately I realized that the terror had been of my own postulation. Corpses do not move. This thing had moved – therefore it was not a corpse, and I had better get hold of myself unless I was determined to go batty.

It was revolting but necessary that I examine the thing. From its fingers thin, fine silver wires led into holes in the slab. I rolled it over, not heeding its terrible groans, and saw that a larger strand penetrated the neck, apparently in contact with its medulla oblongata. Presumably it was sick – this was a hospital. I rambled about cheerfully, scanning cryptic dials on the walls, wondering what would happen next, if anything.

There was a chair facing the wall; I turned it around and sat down.

'Greetings, unknown friend,' said an effeminate voice.

'Greetings right back at you,' said I.

'You have seated yourself in a chair; please be advised that you have set into motion a sound track that may be of interest to you.'

The voice came from a panel in the wall that had lit up with opalescent effects.

'My name,' said the panel, 'is unimportant. You will probably wish to know first, assuming that this record is ever played, that there are duplicates artfully scattered throughout this city, so that whoever visits us will hear our story.'

'Clever, aren't you?' I said sourly. 'Suppose you stop fussing around and tell me what's going on around here.'

'I am speaking,' said the panel, 'from the Fifth Century of Bickerstaff.'

'Whatever that means,' I said.

'Or, by primitive reckoning, 2700 A.D.'

'Thanks.'

'To explain, we must begin at the beginning. You may know that Bickerstaff was a poor Scottish engineer who went and discovered atomic power. I shall pass over his early struggles for recognition, merely stating that the process he invented was economical and efficient beyond anything similar in history.

'With the genius of Bickerstaff as a prod, humanity blossomed forth into its fullest greatness. Poetry and music, architecture and sculpture, letters and graphics became the principal occupations of mankind.'

The panel coughed. 'I myself,' it said, modestly struggling with pride, 'was a composer of no little renown in this city.

'However, there was one thing wrong with the Bickerstaff Power Process. That is, as Bickerstaff was to mankind, so the element yttrium was to his process. It was what is known as a catalyst, a substance introduced into a reaction for the purpose of increasing the speed of the reaction.'

I, a Chemical Engineer, listening to that elementary rot! I didn't walk away. Perhaps he was going to say something of importance.

'In normal reactions the catalyst is not changed either in quantity or in quality, since it takes no real part in the process. However, the Bickerstaff process subjected all matter involved to extraordinary heat, pressure, and bombardment, and so the supply of yttrium has steadily vanished.

'Possibly we should have earlier heeded the warnings of nature. It may be the fault of no one but ourselves that we have allowed our race to become soft and degenerate in the long era of plenty. Power, light, heat – for the asking. And then we faced twin terrors: shortage of yttrium – and the Martians.'

Abruptly I sat straight. Martians! I didn't see any of *them* around.

'Our planetary neighbors,' said the panel, 'are hardly agreeable. It came as a distinct shock to us when their ships landed this year – *my* year, that is – as the bearers of a message.

'Flatly we were ordered: Get out or be crushed. We could have resisted, we could have built war-machines, but what was to power them? Our brain-men did what they could, but it was little enough.

'They warned us, did the Martians. They said that we were worthless, absolutely useless, and they deserved the planet more than we. They had been watching our planet for many years, they said, and we were unfit to own it.

'That is almost a quotation of what they said. Not a translation, either, for they spoke English and indeed all the languages of Earth perfectly. They had observed us so minutely as to learn our tongues!

'Opinion was divided as to the course that lay before us. There were those who claimed that by hoarding the minute supply of yttrium remaining to us we might be able to hold off the invaders when they should come. But while we were discussing the idea the supply was all consumed.

'Some declared themselves for absorption with the Martian race on its arrival. Simple laws of biogenetics demonstrated effectively that such a procedure was likewise impossible.

'A very large group decided to wage guerilla warfare, studying the technique from Clausewitz's "Theory and Practise". Unfortunately, the sole remaining copy of this work crumbled into dust when it was removed from its vault.

'And then . . .

'A man named Selig Vissarion, a poet of Odessa, turned his faculties to the problem, and evolved a device to remove the agonies of waiting. Three months ago – *my* time, remember – he proclaimed it to all mankind.

'His device was – the Biosomniac. It so operates that the sleeper – the subject of the device, that is – is thrown into a deep slumber characterized by dreams of a pleasurable nature. And the slumber is one from which he will never, without outside interference, awake.

'The entire human race, as I speak, is now under the influence of the machine. All but me, and I am left only because there is no one to put me under. When I have done here – I shall shoot myself.

'For this is our tragedy: Now, when all our yttrium is gone, we have found a device to transmute metals. Now we could *make* all the yttrium we need, except that . . .

'*The device cannot be powered except by the destruction of the atom.*

'And, having no yttrium at all left, we can produce no such power . . .

'And so, unknown friend, farewell. You have heard our history. Remember it, and take warning. Be warned of sloth, beware of greed. Farewell, my unknown friend.'

And, with that little sermon, the shifting glow of the panel died and I sat bespelled. It was all a puzzle to me. If the

Martians were coming, why hadn't they arrived? Or had they? At least I saw none about me.

I looked at the mummified figures that stretched in great rows the length of the chamber. These, then, were neither dead nor ill, but sleeping. Sleeping against the coming of the Martians. I thought. My chronology was fearfully confused. Could it be that the invaders from the red planet had not yet come, and that I was only a year or two after the human race had plunged itself into sleep? That must be it.

And all for the want of a little bit of yttrium!

Absently I inspected the appendages of the time travelling belt. They were, for the most part, compact boxes labeled with the curt terminology of engineering. 'Converter,' said one. 'Entropy gradient,' said another. And a third bore the cryptic word, 'Gadenolite.' That baffled my chemical knowledge. Vaguely I remembered *something* I had done back in Housatonic with the stuff. It was a Scandinavian rare earth, as I remember, containing tratia, eunobia, and several oxides, And one of them, I slowly remembered —

Then I said it aloud, with dignity and precision 'One of the compounds present in this earth in large proportions is yttrium dioxide.'

Yttrium dioxide? Why, that was —

Yttrium!

It was one of those things that was just too good to be true. Yttrium! Assuming that the Martians hadn't come yet, and that there really was a decent amount of the metal in the little box on my belt ...

Quite the little heroine, I, I thought cheerfully, and strode to the nearest sleeper. 'Excuse me,' I said.

He groaned as the little reading-lamp flashed on. 'Excuse me,' I said again.

He didn't move. Stern measures seemed to be called for. I shouted in his ear, 'Wake up, you!' But he wouldn't.

I wandered among the sleepers, trying to arouse some, and

failing in every case. It must be those little wires, I thought gaily as I bent over one of them.

I inspected the hand of the creature, and noted that the silvery filaments trailing from the fingers did not seem to be imbedded very deeply in the flesh. Taking a deep breath I twisted one of the wires between forefinger and thumb, and broke it with ease.

The creature groaned again, and – opened its eyes!

'Good morning,' I said feebly.

It didn't answer me, but sat up and stared from terribly sunken pits for a full second. It uttered a little wailing cry. The eyes closed again, and the creature rolled from its slab, falling heavily to the floor. I felt for the pulse; there was none. Beyond doubt this sleeper slept no longer – I had killed him.

I walked away from the spot, realizing that my problem was not as simple as it might have been. A faint glow lit up the hall, and the lights above flashed out. The new radiance came through the walls of the building.

It must be morning, I thought. I had had a hard night, and a strange one. I pressed the 'Slavies' ring' again, and took the revolving staircase down to the lobby.

The thing to do now was to find some way of awakening the sleepers without killing them. That meant study. Study meant books, books meant library. I walked out into the polished stone plaza and looked for libraries.

There was some fruitless wandering about and stumbling into several structures precisely similar to the one I had visited; finally down the vista of a broad, gleaming street I saw the deep-carven words, 'Stape Books Place,' on the pediment of a traditionally squat, classic building. I set off for it, and arrived too winded by the brisk walk to do anything more than throw myself into a chair.

A panel in the wall lit up and an effeminate voice began, 'Greetings, unknown friend. You have seated yourself in a chair; please be advised —'

'Go to hell,' I said shortly, rose, and left the panel to go through a door inscribed 'Books of the Day.'

It turned out to be a conventional reading room whose farther end was a maze of stacks and shelves. Light poured in through large windows, and I felt homesick for old Housatonic. If the place had been a little more dusty I'd never have known it from the Main Tech Library.

A volume I chose at random proved to be a work on anthropology: 'A General Introduction to the Study of Decapilation Among the Tertiates of Gondwana as Contrasted with the Primates of Eurasia.' I found one photograph – in color – of a hairless monkey, shuddered, and restored the volume.

The next book was 'The Exagmination into the incamination for the resons of his Works in pregreSs,' which also left me stranded. It appeared to be a critique of the middle work of one James Joyce, reprinted from the original edition of Paris, 1934 A.D.

I chucked the thing into a corner and rummaged among the piles of pamphlets that jammed a dozen shelves. 'Rittenhouse's Necrology' – no. 'Statistical Isolates Relating to Isolate Statisticals' – likewise no. 'The Cognocrat Manifest' – I opened it and found it a description of a super-state which had yet to be created. 'Construction and operation of the Biosomniac' – that was it!

I seated myself at one of the polished tables and read through the slim pamphlet rapidly once, then tore out some of its blank pages to take notes on. 'The arrangement of the regulating dials is optional,' I copied on to the paper scraps, and sketched the intricate system of Bowden wires that connected the bodies with the controls. That was as much of a clue as I could get from the little volume, but it indicated in its appendix more exhaustive works. I looked up 'Vissarion,' the first on the list.

'Monarch! may many moiling mockers make
my master more malicious marry mate —'

it said. Mankind, artist to the last, had yet found time to compose an epic poem on the inventor of the Biosomniac. I flung the sappy thing away and took down the next work on the list, 'Chemistry of the Somniac.' It was a sound treatise on the minute yet perceptible functionings of the subject under the influence of the Vissarion device. More notes and diagrams, collated with the information from the other book.

'The vitality of the sleeper is most profoundly affected by the operations of the Alphate dial ... It is believed that the Somniac may be awakened by a suitable manipulation of the ego-flow so calculated as to stock the sleeper to survive a severing of the quasi-amniotic wiring system.'

I rose and tucked the notes into my belt. That was enough for me! I'd have to experiment, and most likely make a few mistakes, but in a few hours men would be awake to grow hard and strong again after their long sleep, to pluck out their wires themselves, and to take my yttrium and with it build the needed war-machines against the Martians. No more sleep for Earth! And perhaps a new flowering of life when the crisis of the invaders was past?

'The compleat heroine – quite!' I chortled aloud as I passed through the door. I glanced at the glowing panel, but it glowed no longer – the unknown speaker had said his piece and was done. Onward and outward to save the world, I thought.

'Excuse me,' said a voice.

I spun around and saw a fishy individual staring at me through what seemed to be a small window.

'What are you doing awake?' I asked excitedly.

He laughed softly. 'That, my dear young lady, is just what I was about to ask you.'

'Come out from behind that window,' I said nervously. 'I can hardly see you.'

'Don't be silly,' he said sharply. 'I'm quite a few million miles away. I'm on Mars. In fact, I'm a Martian.'

I looked closer. He *did* seem sort of peculiar, but hardly the bogey-man that his race had been cracked up to be. 'Then you will please tell me what you want,' I said. 'I'm a busy woman with little time to waste on Martians.' Brave words. I knew it would take him a while to get from Mars to where I was; by that time I would have everyone awake and stinging.

'Oh,' he said casually. 'I just thought you might like a little chat. I suppose you're a time-traveller.'

'Just that.'

'I thought so. You're the fourth – no, the fifth – this week. Funny how they always seem to hit on this year. My name is Alfred, John Alfred.'

'How do you do?' I said politely. 'And I'm Mabel Evans of Colchester, Vermont. Year, 1940. But why have you got a name like an Earthman?'

'We all have,' he answered. 'We copied it from you Terrestrials. It's your major contribution to our culture.'

'I suppose so,' I said bitterly. 'Those jellyfish didn't have much to offer anybody except poetry and bad sculpture. I hardly know why I'm reviving them and giving them the yttrium to fight you blokes off.'

He looked bored, as nearly as I could see. 'Oh, have you some yttrium?'

'Yes.'

'Much?'

'Enough for a start. Besides, I expect them to pick up and acquire some independence once they get through their brush-up with Mars. By the way – when will you invade?'

'We plan to *colonize*,' he said, delicately emphasizing the word, 'beginning about two years from now. It will take that long to get everything in shape to move.'

'That's fine,' I said enthusiastically. 'We should have plenty of time to get ready, I think. What kind of weapons do you use? Death-rays?'

'Of course,' said the Martian. 'And heat rays, and molecular collapse rays, and disintegrator rays, and resistance rays – you just call it and we have it in stock, lady.'

He was a little boastful. 'Well,' I said, 'you just wait until we get a few factories going – *then* you'll see what high-speed, high-grade production can be. We'll have everything you've got – double.'

'All this, of course,' he said with a smug smile, 'after you wake the sleepers and give them your yttrium?'

'Of course. Why shouldn't it be?'

'Oh, I was just asking. But I have an idea that you've made a fundamental error.'

'Error my neck,' I said. 'What do you mean?'

'Listen closely, please,' he said. 'Your machine – that is, your time-traveller – operates on the principle of similar circles, does it not?'

'I *seem* to remember that it does. So what?'

'So this, Miss Evans. You postulate that firstly the circumference of all circles equals infinity times zero. Am I right?'

That was approximately what Stephen had said, so I supposed that he was. 'Right as rarebits,' I said.

'Now, your further hypothesis is probably that all circles are equal. And that equal distances traversed at equal speeds are traversed in equal times. Am I still right?'

'That seemed to be the idea.'

'Very well.' A smug smile broke over his fishy face. He continued. 'Your theory works beautifully – but your machine – no.'

I looked down at myself to see if I were there. I was.

'Explain that, please,' I said. 'Why doesn't the machine work?'

'For this reason. Infinity times zero does *not* equal *a* number. It equals *any* number. A definite number is represented by x; *any* number, n. See the difference? And so unequal circles are still unequal, and cannot be circumnavigated as of the same distance at the same speed in the same time. And your theory – is a fallacy.'

He looked at me gloatingly before continuing. Then, slowly, 'Your theory is fallacious. Ergo, your machine doesn't work. If your machine doesn't work, you couldn't have used it to get here. There is no other way for you to have gotten here. Therefore ... *you are not here!* and so the projected *colonization* will proceed on schedule!'

And the light flashed in my head. Of course! that was what I had been trying to think of back in the house. The weakness in Trainer's logic!

Then I went *pouf* again, my eyes closed, and I thought to myself, 'Since the machine didn't work and couldn't have worked, I didn't travel in time. So I must be back with Trainer.'

I opened my eyes. I was.

'You moron,' I snapped at him as he stood goggle-eyed, his hand on the wall-socket. 'Your machine doesn't work!'

He stared at me blankly. 'You were gone. Where were you?'

'It seemed to be 2700 A.D.,' I answered.

'How was it?' he inquired, reaching for a fresh flask of ethyl.

'Very, very silly. I'm glad the machine didn't work.' He offered me a beaker and I drained it. 'I'd hate to think that I'd really been there.' I took off the belt and stretched my aching muscles.

'Do you know, Mabel,' he said, looking at me hard, 'I think I'm going to like this town.'

It was very simple. Some combination of low temperature and high pressure had forced something from the seepage at the ocean bottom into combination with something in the water around them.

And the impregnable armor around Subatlantic Oil's drilling chamber had discovered a weakness.

On the television screen it looked more serious than it was – so Muhlenhoff told himself, staring at it grimly. You get down more than a mile, and you're bound to have little technical problems. That's why deepsea oil wells were still there.

Still, it did look kind of serious. The water driving in the pitted faults had the pressure of eighteen hundred meters behind it, and where it struck it did not splash – it battered and destroyed. As Muhlenhoff watched, a bulkhead collapsed in an explosion of spray; the remote camera caught a tiny driblet of the scattering brine, and the picture in the screen fluttered and shrank, and came back with a wavering sidewise pulse.

Muhlenhoff flicked off the screen and marched into the room where the Engineering Board was waiting in attitudes of flabby panic.

As he swept his hand through his snow-white crew cut and called the board to order a dispatch was handed to him – a preliminary report from a quickly-dispatched company troubleshooter team. He read it to the board, stone-faced.

A veteran heat-transfer man, the first to recover, growled:

'Some vibration thing – and seepage from the oil pool. Sloppy drilling!' He sneered. 'Big deal! So a couple hundred meters of shaft have to be plugged and pumped. So six or eight compartments go pop. Since when did we start to believe the cack Research & Development hands out? Armor's armor. Sure it pops – when something makes it pop. If Atlantic oil was easy to get at, it wouldn't be here waiting for us now. Put a gang on the job. Find out what happened, make sure it doesn't happen again. Big deal!'

Muhlenhoff smiled his attractive smile. 'Breck,' he said, 'thank God you've got guts. Perhaps we were in a bit of a panic. Gentlemen, I hope we'll all take heart from Mr. Breck's level-headed – what did you say, Breck?'

Breck didn't look up. He was pawing through the dispatch Muhlenhoff had dropped to the table. 'Nine-inch plate,' he read aloud, white-faced. 'And time of installation, not quite seven weeks ago. If this goes on in a straight line —' he grabbed for a pocket slide-rule – 'we have, uh —' he swallowed – 'less time than the probable error,' he finished.

'Breck!' Muhlenhoff yelled. 'Where are you going?'

The veteran heat-transfer man said grimly as he sped through the door: 'To find a submarine.'

The rest of the Engineering Board was suddenly pulling chairs toward the trouble-shooting team's dispatch. Muhlenhoff slammed a fist on the table.

'Stop it,' he said evenly. 'The next man who leaves the meeting will have his contract canceled. Is that clear, gentlemen? Good. We will now proceed to get organized.'

He had them; they were listening. He said forcefully: 'I want a task force consisting of a petrochemist, a vibrations man, a hydrostatics man and a structural engineer. Co-opt mathematicians and computermen as needed. I will have all machines capable of handling Fourier series and up cleared for your use. The work of the task force will be divided into two phases. For Phase One, members will keep their staffs as small as possible. The objective of Phase One is to find the cause of the leaks and predict whether similar leaks are likely elsewhere in the project. On receiving a first approximation from the force I will proceed to set up Phase Two, to deal with countermeasures.'

He paused. 'Gentlemen,' he said, 'we must not lose our nerves. We must not panic. Possibly the most serious technical crisis in Atlantic's history lies before us. Your most important job is to maintain – at all times – a cheerful, courageous attitude. We cannot, repeat cannot, afford to have the sub-technical staff of the project panicked for lack of a good example from us.' He drilled each of them in turn with a long glare. 'And,' he finished, 'if I hear of anyone suddenly discovering emergency business ashore, the man who does it better get fitted for a sludgemonkey's suit, because that's what he'll be tomorrow. Clear?'

Each of the executives assumed some version of a cheerful, courageous attitude. They looked ghastly, even to themselves.

Muhlenhoff stalked into his private office, the nerve-center of the whole bulkheaded works.

In Muhlenhoff's private office, you would never know you were 1800 meters below the surface of the sea. It looked like any oilman's brass-hat office anywhere, complete to the beautiful blonde outside the door (but white-faced and trembling), the potted palm (though the ends of its fronds vibrated gently), and the typical section chief bursting in in the typical flap. 'Sir,' he whined, frenzied, 'Section Six has pinholed! The corrosion —'

'Handle it!' barked Muhlenhoff, and slammed the door. Section Six be damned! What did it matter if a few of the old bulkheads pinholed and filled? The central chambers were safe, until they could lick whatever it was that was corroding. The point was, you had to stay with it and get out the oil; because if you didn't prove your lease, PetroMex would. Mexican oil wanted those reserves mighty badly.

Muhlenhoff knew how to handle an emergency. Back away from it. Get a fresh slant. Above all, *don't panic*.

He slapped a button that guaranteed no interruption and irritably, seeking distraction, picked up his latest copy of the *New New Review* – for he was, among other things, an intellectual as time allowed.

Under the magazine was the latest of several confidential communications from the home office. Muhlenhoff growled and tossed the magazine aside. He reread what Priestley had

had to say:

'I know you understand the importance of beating our Spic friends to the Atlantic deep reserves, so I won't give you a hard time about it. I'll just pass it on the way Lundstrom gave it to me: "Tell Muhlenhoff he'll come back on the Board or on a board, and no alibis or excuses." Get it? Well—'

Hell. Muhlenhoff threw the sheet down and tried to think about the damned corrosion-leakage situation.

But he didn't try for long. There was, he realized, no point at all in him thinking about the problem. For one thing, he no longer had the equipment.

Muhlenhoff realized, wonderingly, that he hadn't opened a table of integrals for ten years; he doubted that he could find his way around the pages well enough to run down a tricky form. He had come up pretty fast through the huge technical staff of Atlantic. First he had been a geologist in the procurement section, one of those boots-and-leather jacket guys who spent his days in rough, tough blasting and drilling and his nights in rarefied scientific air, correlating and integrating the findings of the day. Next he had been a Chief Geologist, chairborne director of youngsters, now and then tackling a muddled report with Theory of Least Squares and Gibbs Phase Rule that magically separated dross from limpid fact ... or, he admitted wryly, at least turning the muddled reports over to mathematicians who specialized in those disciplines.

Next he had been a Raw Materials Committee member who knew that drilling and figuring weren't the almighty things he had supposed them when he was a kid, who began to see the Big Picture of off-shore leases and depreciation allowances; of power and fusible rocks and steel for the machines, butane for the drills, plastics for the pipelines, metals for the circuits, the computers, the doors, windows, walls, tools, utilities. A committeeman who began to see that a friendly beer poured for the right resources-commission man was really more important than Least Squares or Phase Rule, because a resources commissioner who didn't get along with you might get along, for instance, with somebody from Coastwide, and allot to Coastwide the next available block of leases – thus working grievous harm to Atlantic and the billions it served. A committeeman who began to see that the Big Picture meant government and science leaning chummily against each other, government setting science new and challenging tasks like the billion-barrel procurement program, science backing government with all its tremendous prestige. You consume my waste hydrocarbons, Muhlenhoff thought comfortably, and I'll consume yours.

Thus mined, smelted and milled, Muhlenhoff was tempered for higher things. For the first, the technical directorate of an entire Atlantic Sub-Sea Petroleum Corporation district, and all wells, fields, pipelines, stills, storage fields, transport, fabrication and maintenance appertaining thereto. Honors piled upon honors. And then—

He glanced around him at the comfortable office. The top. Nothing to be added but voting stock and Board membership – and those within his grasp, if only he weathered this last crisis. And then the rarefield height he occupied alone.

And, by God, he thought, I do a damn good job of it! Pleasurably he reviewed his conduct at the meeting; he had already forgotten his panic. Those shaking fools would have brought the roof down on us, he thought savagely. A few gallons of water in an unimportant shaft, and they're set to message the home office, run for the surface, abandon the whole project. The Big Picture! They didn't see it, and they never would. He might, he admitted, not be able to chase an integral form through a table, but by God he could give the orders to those who would. The thing was organized now; the project was rolling; the task force had its job mapped out; and somehow, although he would not do a jot of the brain-wearing, eyestraining, actual work, it would be *his* job, because he had initiated it. He thought of the flat, dark square miles of calcareous ooze outside, under which lay the biggest proved untapped petroleum reserve in the world. Sector Fortyone, it was called on the hydrographic charts.

Perhaps, some day, the charts would say: *Muhlenhoff Basin*.

Well, why not?

The emergency intercom was flickering its red call light pusillanimously. Muhlenhoff calmly lifted the handset off its cradle and ignored the tinny bleat. When you gave an order, you had to leave the men alone to carry it out.

He relaxed his chair and picked up a book from the desk. He was, among other things, a student of Old American History, as time permitted.

Fifteen minutes now, he promised himself, with the heroic past. And then back to work refreshed!

Muhlenhoff plunged into the book. He had schooled himself to concentration; he hardly noticed when the pleading noise from the intercom finally gave up trying to attract his attention. The book was a study of that Mexican War in which the United States had been so astonishingly deprived of Texas, Oklahoma and points west under the infamous Peace of Galveston. The story was well told; Muhlenhoff was lost in its story from the first page.

Good thumbnail sketch of Presidente Lopez, artistically contrasted with the United States' Whitmore. More-in-sorrow-than-in-anger off-the-cuff psychoanalysis of the crackpot Texan Byerly, derisively known to Mexicans as 'El Cacafuego.' Byerly's raid at the head of his screwball irredentists, their prompt annihilation by the Mexican Third Armored Regiment, Byerly's impeccably legal trial and execution at Tehuantepec. Stiff diplomatic note from the United States. Bland answer: Please mind your business, Señores, and we will mind ours. Stiffer diplomatic note. We said *please*, Señores, and can we not let it go at that? *Very* stiff diplomatic note; and Latin temper flares at last: Mexico severs relations.

Bad to worse. Worse to worst.

Massacre of Mexican nationals at San Antonio. Bland refusal of the United States federal government to interfere in 'local police problem' of punishing the guilty. Mexican Third Armored raids San Antone, arrests the murderers (feted for weeks, their faces in the papers, their proud boasts of butchery retold everywhere), and hangs them before recrossing the border.

United States declares war. United States loses war – outmaneuvered, outgeneraled, out-logisticated, outgunned, outmanned.

And outfought.

Said the author:

'The colossal blow this cold military fact delivered to the United States collective ego is inconceivable to us today. Only a study of contemporary comment can make it real to the historian: The choked hysteria of the newspapers, the raging tides of suicides, Whitmore's impeachment and trial, the forced resignations of the entire General Staff – all these serve only to sketch in the national mood.

'Clearly something has happened to the military power which, within less than five decades previous, had annihilated the war machines of the Cominform and the Third Reich.

'We have the words of the contemporary military analyst, Osgood Ferguson, to explain it:

'The rise of the so-called "political general" means a decline in the efficiency of the army. Other things being equal, an undistracted professional beats an officer who is half soldier and half politician. A general who makes it his sole job to win a war will infallibly defeat an opponent who, by choice or constraint, must offend no voters of enemy ancestry, destroy no cultural or religious shrines highly regarded by the press, show leniency when leniency is fashionable at home, display condign firmness when voters demand it (though it cause his zone of communications to blaze up into a fury of guerrilla clashes), choose his invasion routes to please a state department apprehensive of potential future ententes.

'It is unfortunate that most of Ferguson's documentation was lost when his home was burned during the unsettled years after the war. But we know that what Mexico's Presidente Lopez said to his staff was: "My generals, win me this war." And this entire volume does not have enough space to record what the United States generals were told by the White House, the Congress as a whole, the Committees on Military Affairs, the Special Committees on Conduct of the War, the State Department, the Commerce Department, the Interior Department, the Director of the Budget, the War Manpower Commission, the Republican National Committee, the Democratic National Committee, the Steel lobby, the Oil lobby, the Labor lobby, the political journals, the daily newspapers, the broadcasters, the ministry, the Granges, the Chambers of Commerce. However, we do know – unhappily – that the United States generals obeyed their orders. This sorry fact was inscribed indelibly on the record at the Peace of Galveston.'

Muhlenhoff yawned and closed the book. An amusing theory, he thought, but thin. Political generals? Nonsense.

He was glad to see that his subordinates had given up their attempt to pass responsibility for the immediate problem to his shoulders; the intercom had been silent for many minutes now. It only showed, he thought comfortably, that they had absorbed his leading better than they knew.

He glanced regretfully at the door that had sheltered him, for this precious refreshing interlude, from the shocks of the project outside. Well, the interlude was over; now to see about this leakage thing. Muhlenhoff made a note, in his tidy card-catalog mind, to have Maintenance on the carpet. The door was bulging out of true. Incredible sloppiness! And some damned fool had shut the locks in the ventilating system. The air was becoming stuffy.

Aggressive and confident, the political engineer pressed the release that opened the door to the greatest shock of all.

Mars-Tube

I

After Armageddon

Ray Stanton set his jaw as he stared at the molded lead seal on the museum door. Slowly, he deciphered its inscription, his tongue stumbling over the unfamiliar sibilants of the Martian language as he read it aloud before translating. 'To the – strangers from the third planet – who have won their – bitter – triumph – we of Mars charge you, – not to wantonly destroy – that which you will find – within this door ... Our codified learning – may serve you – better than we ourselves – might have done.'

Stanton was ashamed of being an Earthman as he read this soft indictment. 'Pathetic,' he whispered. 'Those poor damned people.'

His companion, a slight, dark-haired girl who seemed out of place in the first exploratory expedition to visit Mars after the decades-long war that had annihilated its population, nodded in agreement. 'The war was a crying shame,' she confirmed. 'But mourning the dead won't bring them back. To work, Stanton!'

Stanton shook his head dolefully, but copied the seal's inscription into his voluminous black archaeologist's notebook. Then he tore off the seal and tentatively pushed the door. It swung open easily, and an automatic switch snapped on the hidden lights as the two people entered.

Both Stanton and Annamarie Hudgins, the girl librarian of the expedition, had seen many marvels in their wanderings over and under the red planet, for every secret place was open to their eyes. But as the lights slowly blossomed over the colossal hall of the library, he staggered back in amazement that so much stately glory could be built into one room.

The synthetic slabs of gem-like rose crystal that the Martians had reserved for their most awesome sanctuaries were flashing from every wall and article of furnishing, winking with soft ruby lights. One of the typically Martian ramps led up in a gentle curve from their left. The practical Annamarie at once commenced to mount it, heading for the reading-rooms that would be found above. Stanton followed more slowly, pausing to examine the symbolic ornamentation in the walls.

'We must have guessed right, Annamarie,' he observed, catching up with her. 'This one's the central museum-library for sure. Take a look at the wall-motif.'

Annamarie glanced at a panel just ahead, a bas-relief done in the rose crystal. 'Because of the *ultima* symbol, you mean?'

'Yes, and because – well, look.' The room in which they found themselves was less noble than the other, but considerably more practical. It was of radical design, corridors converging like the spokes of a wheel on a focal point where they stood. Inset in the floor – they were almost standing on it – was the *ultima* symbol, the quadruple linked circles which indicated pre-eminence. Stanton peered down a corridor lined with racks of wire spools. He picked up a spool and stared at its title-tag.

'Where do you suppose we ought to start?' he asked.

'Anywhere at all,' Annamarie replied. 'We've got lots of time, and no way of knowing what to look for. What's the one in your hands?'

'It seems to say, "The Under-Eaters" – whatever that may mean,' Stanton juggled the tiny 'book' undecidedly. 'That phrase seems familiar somehow. What is it?'

'Couldn't say. Put it in the scanner and we'll find out.' Stanton obeyed, pulling a tiny reading-machine from its cubicle. The delicacy with which Stanton threaded the fragile wire into its proper receptacle was something to watch. The party had ruined a hundred spools of records before they'd learned how to adjust the scanners, and Stanton had learned caution.

Stanton and his companion leaned back against the book-racks and watched the fluorescent screen of the scanner. A touch of the lever started its operation. There was a soundless flare of light on the screen as the wire made contact with the scanning apparatus, then the screen filled with the curious wavering peak-and-valley writing of the Martian graphic language.

By the end of the third 'chapter' the title of the book was still almost as cryptic as ever. A sort of preface had indicated that 'Under-Eaters' was a name applied to a race of underground demons who feasted on the flesh of living Martians. Whether these really existed or not Stanton had no way of telling. The Martians had made no literary distinction between fact and fiction, as far as could be learned. It had been their opinion that anything except pure thought-transference was only approximately true, and that it would be useless to distinguish between an intentional and an unintentional falsehood.

But the title had no bearing on the context of the book, which was a kind of pseudo-history with heavily allusive passages. It treated of the Earth-Mars war: seemingly it had been published only a few months before the abrupt end to hostilities. One rather tragic passage, so Stanton thought, read:

'A special meeting of the tactical council was called on (an untranslatable date) to discuss the so-called new disease on which the attention of the enemy forces has been concentrating. This was argued against by (a high official) who demonstrated conclusively that the Martian intellect was immune to nervous diseases of any foreign order, due to its high development through telepathy as cultivated for (an untranslatable number of) generations. A minority report submitted that this very development itself would render the Martian intellect more liable to succumb to unusual strain. (A medical authority) suggested that certain forms of insanity were contagious by means of telepathy, and that the enemy-spread disease might be of that type.'

Stanton cursed softly: 'Damn Moriarity and his rocket ship. Damn Sweeney for getting killed and damn and double-damn the World Congress for declaring war on Mars!' He felt like a murderer, though he knew he was no more than a slightly pacifistic young exploring archaeologist. Annamarie nodded sympathetically but pointed at the screen. Stanton looked again and his imprecations were forgotten as he brought his mind to the problem of translating another of the strangely referential passages:

'At this time the Under-Eaters launched a bombing campaign on several of the underground cities. A number of sub-terranean-caves were linked with the surface through explosion craters and many of the sinister creations fumbled their way to the surface. A corps of technologists prepared to re-seal the tunnels of the Revived, which was done with complete success, save only in (an untranslatable place-name) where several Under-Eaters managed to wreak great havoc before being slain or driven back to their tunnels. The ravages of the Twice-Born, however, were trivial compared to the deaths resulting from the mind diseases fostered by the flying ships of the Under-Eaters, which were at this time . . .'

The archaeologist frowned. There it was again. Part of the time 'Under-Eaters' obviously referred to the Earthmen, the rest of the time it equally obviously did not. The text would limp along in styleless, concise prose and then in would break an obscure reference to the 'Creations' or 'Twice-Born' or 'Raging Glows.'

'Fairy tales for the kiddies,' said Annamarie Hudgins, snapping off the scanner.

Stanton replied indirectly: 'Put it in the knapsack. I want to take it back and show it to some of the others. Maybe they can tell me what it means.' He swept a handful of other reading-bobbins at random into the knapsack, snapped it shut, and straightened. 'Lead on, Mac-Hudgins,' he said.

Of the many wonders of the red planet, the one that the exploration party had come to appreciate most was the colossal system of subways which connected each of the underground cities of Mars.

With absolute precision the web of tunnels and gliding cars still functioned, and would continue to do so until the central controls were found by some Earthman and the vast propulsive mechanisms turned off.

The Mars-Tube was electrostatic in principle. The perfectly round tunnels through which the subway sped were studded with hoops of charged metal. The analysis of the metal hoops and the generators for the propulsive force had been beyond Earthly science, at least as represented by the understaffed exploring party.

Through these hoops sped the single-car trains of the Mars-Tube, every four minutes through every hour of the long Martian day. The electrostatic emanations from the hoops held the cars nicely balanced against the pull of gravity; save only when they stopped for the stations, the cars never touched anything more substantial than a puff of air. The average speed of the subway, stops not included, was upwards of five hundred miles an hour. There were no windows in the cars, for there would have been nothing to see through them but the endless tunnel wall slipping smoothly and silently by.

So easy was the completely automatic operation that the men from Earth could scarcely tell when the car was in motion, except by the signal panel that dominated one end of the car with its blinking lights and numerals.

Stanton led Annamarie to a station with ease and assurance. There was only one meaning to the tear-drop-shaped guide signs of a unique orange color that were all over Mars. Follow the point of a sign like that anywhere on Mars and you'd find yourself at a Mars-Tube station – or what passed for one.

Since there was only one door to a car, and that opened automatically whenever the car stopped at a station, there were no platforms. Just a smaller or larger anteroom with a door also opening automatically, meeting the door of the tube-car.

A train eventually slid in, and Stanton ushered Annamarie through the sliding doors. They swung themselves gently on to one of the excessively broad seats and immediately opened their notebooks. Each seat had been built for a single Martian, but accommodated two Terrestrials with room to spare.

At perhaps the third station, Annamarie, pondering the implications of a passage in the notebook, looked up for an abstracted second – and froze. 'Ray,' she whispered in a strangled tone. 'When did that come in?'

Stanton darted a glance at the forward section of the car, which they had ignored when entering. Something – something animate – was sitting there, quite stolidly ignoring the Terrestrials. 'A Martian,' he whispered to himself, his throat dry.

It had the enormous chest and hips, the waspish waist and the coarse, bristly hairs of the Martians. But the Martians were all dead —

'It's only a robot,' he cried more loudly than was necessary, swallowing as he spoke. 'Haven't you seen enough of them to know what they look like by now?'

'What's it doing here?' gulped Annamarie, not over the fright.

As though it were about to answer her question itself, the thing's metallic head turned, and its blinking eyes swept incuriously over the humans. For a long second it stared, then the dull glow within its eye-sockets faded, and the head turned again to the front. The two had not set off any system of reflexes in the creature.

'I never saw one of them in the subway before,' said Annamarie, passing a damp hand over her sweating brow.

Stanton was glaring at the signal panel that dominated the front of the car. 'I know why, too,' he said. 'I'm not as good a linguist as I thought I was – not even as good as I ought to be. We're on the wrong train – I read the code-symbol wrong.'

Annamarie giggled. 'Then what shall we do – see where this takes us or go back?'

'Get out and go back, of course,' grumbled Stanton, rising and dragging her to her feet.

The car was slowing again for another station. They could get out, emerge to the surface, cross over, and take the return train to the library.

Only the robot wouldn't let them.

For as the car was slowing, the robot rose to its feet and stalked over to the door. 'What's up?' Stanton whispered in a thin, nervous voice. Annamarie prudently got behind him.

'We're getting out here anyhow,' she said. 'Maybe it won't follow us.'

But they didn't get out. For when the car had stopped, and the door relays clicked, the robot shouldered the humans aside and stepped to the door.

But instead of exiting himself, the robot grasped the edge of the door in his steel tentacles, clutched it with all his metal muscles straining, and held it shut!

'Damned if I can understand it,' said Stanton. 'It was the most uncanny thing – it held the door completely and totally shut there, but it let us get out as peaceful as playmates at the next stop. We crossed over to come back, and while we were waiting for a return car I had time to dope out the station number. It was seventh from the end of the line, and the branch was new to me. So we took the return car back to the museum. The same thing happened on the trip back – robot in the car; door held shut.'

'Go on,' said Ogden Josey, Roëntgenologist of the expedition. 'What happened then?'

'Oh. We just went back to the library, took a different car, and here we are.'

'Interesting,' said Josey. 'Only I don't believe it a bit.'

'No?' Annamarie interrupted, her eyes narrowing. 'Want to take a look?'

'Sure.'

'How about tomorrow morning?'

'Fine,' said Josey. 'You can't scare me. Now how about dinner?'

He marched into the mess hall of the expedition base, a huge rotunda-like affair that might have been designed for anything by the Martians, but was given its present capacity by the explorers because it contained tables and chairs enough for a regiment. Stanton and Annamarie lagged behind.

'What do you plan to do tomorrow?' Stanton inquired. 'I don't see the point of taking Josey with us when we go to look the situation over again.'

'He'll come in handy,' Annamarie promised. 'He's a good shot.'

'A good shot?' squawked Stanton. 'What do you expect we'll have to shoot at?'

But Annamarie was already inside the building.

II

Descent into Danger

'Hey, sand-man!' hissed Annamarie.

'Be right there,' sleepily said Stanton. 'This is the strangest date I ever had.' He appeared a moment later dressed in the roughest kind of exploring kit.

The girl raised her brows. 'Expect to go mountain-climbing?' she asked.

'I had a hunch,' he said amiably.

'So?' she commented. 'I get them too. One of them is that Josey is still asleep. Go rout him out.'

Stanton grinned and disappeared into Josey's cubicle, emerging with him a few moments later. 'He was sleeping in his clothes,' Stanton explained. 'Filthy habit.'

'Never mind that. Are we all heeled?' Annamarie proudly displayed her own pearl-handled pipsqueak of a mild paralyzer. Joseph produced a heat-pistol, while Stanton patted the holster of his five-pound blaster.

'Okay then. We're off.'

The Martian subway service was excellent every hour of the day. Despite the earliness, the trip to the central museum station took no more time than usual – a matter of minutes.

Stanton stared around for a second to get his bearings, then pointed. 'The station we want is over there – just beyond the large pink monolith. Let's go.'

The first train in was the one they wanted. They stepped into it, Josey leaping over the threshold like a startled fawn. Nervously he explained, 'I never know when one of those things is going to snap shut on my – my cape.' He yelped shrilly: 'What's *that*?'

'Ah, I see the robots rise early,' said Annamarie, seating herself as the train moved off. 'Don't look so disturbed, Josey – we told you one would be here, even if you didn't believe us.'

'We have just time for a spot of breakfast before things should happen,' announced Stanton, drawing canisters from a pouch on his belt. 'Here – one for each of us.' They were filled with a syrup that the members of the Earth expedition carried on trips such as this – concentrated amino acids, fibrinogen, minerals and vitamins, all in a sugar solution.

Annamarie Hudgins shuddered as she downed the sticky stuff, then lit a cigarette. As the lighter flared the robot turned his head to precisely the angle required to center and focus its eyes on the flame, then eye-fronted again.

'Attracted by light and motion,' Stanton advised scientifically. 'Stop trembling, Josey, there's worse to come. Say, is this the station?'

'It is,' said Annamarie. 'Now watch. These robots function smoothly and fast – don't miss anything.'

The metal monster, with a minimum of waste motion, was doing just that. It had clumped over to the door; its monstrous appendages were fighting the relays that were to drive the door open, and the robot was winning. The robots were built to win – powerful, even by Earthly standards.

Stanton rubbed his hands briskly and tackled the robot, shoving hard. The girl laughed sharply. He turned, his face showing injury. 'Suppose you help,' he suggested with some anger. 'I can't move this by myself.'

'All right – heave!' gasped the girl, complying.

'Ho!' added Josey unexpectedly, adding his weight.

'No use,' said Stanton. 'No use at all. We couldn't move this thing in seven million years.' He wiped his brow. The train started, then picked up speed. All three were thrown back as the robot carelessly nudged them out of its way as it returned to its seat.

'I think,' said Josey abruptly, 'we'd better go back by the return car and see about the other side of the station.'

'No use,' said the girl. 'There's a robot on the return, too.'

'Then let's walk back,' urged Josey. By which time the car had stopped at the next station. 'Come on,' said Josey, stepping through the door with a suspicious glance at the robot.

'No harm in trying,' mused Stanton as he followed with the girl. 'Can't be more than twenty miles.'

'And that's easier than twenty Earth miles,' cried Annamarie. 'Let's go.'

'I don't know what good it will do though,' remarked Stanton, ever the pessimist. 'These Martians were thorough. There's probably a robot at every entrance to the station, blocking the way. *If* they haven't sealed up the entrances entirely.'

There was no robot at the station, they discovered several hours and about eight miles later. But the entrance to the station that was so thoroughly and mysteriously guarded was – no more. Each entrance was sealed; only the glowing teardrop pointers remained to show where the entrance had been.

'Well, what do we do now?' groaned Josey, rubbing an aching thigh.

Stanton did not answer directly. 'Will you look at that,' he marvelled, indicating the surrounding terrain. The paved ground beneath them was seamed with cracks. The infinitely tough construction concrete of the Martians was billowed and rippled, stuck through with jagged ends of metal reinforcing I-beams. The whole scene gave the appearance of total devastation – as though a natural catastrophe had come along and wrecked the city first; then the survivors of the disaster, petulantly, had turned their most potent forces on what was left in sheer disheartenment.

'Must have been bombs,' suggested the girl.

'Must have been,' agreed the archaeologist. 'Bombs and guns and force beams and Earth – Marsquakes, too.'

'You didn't answer his question, Ray,' reminded Annamarie. 'He said: "What do we do now?"'

'I was just thinking about it,' he said, eyeing one of the monolithic buildings speculatively. 'Is your Martian as good as mine? See if you can make out what that says.'

'That' was a code-symbol over the sole door to the huge edifice. 'I give up,' said Annamarie with irritation. 'What does it say?'

'Powerhouse, I think.'

'Powerhouse? Powerhouse for what? All the energy for lighting and heating the city comes from the sun, through the mirrors up on the surface. The only thing they need power for down here – the only thing – Say!'

'That's right,' grinned Stanton. 'It must be for the Mars-Tube. Do you suppose we could find a way of getting from that building into the station?'

'There's only one way to find out,' Annamarie parroted, looking for Josey for confirmation. But Josey was no longer around. He was at the door to the building, shoving it open. The others hastened after him.

III

Pursuit

'Don't wiggle, Annamarie,' whispered Josey plaintively. 'You'll fall on me.'

'Shut up,' she answered tersely; 'shut up and get out of my way.' She swung herself down the Martian-sized manhole with space to spare. Dropping three feet or so from her hand-hold on the lip of the pit, she alighted easily. 'Did I make much noise?' she asked.

'Oh, I think Krakatoa has been louder when it went off,' Stanton replied bitterly. 'But those things seem to be deaf.'

The three stood perfectly still for a second, listening tensely for sounds of pursuit. They had stumbled into a nest of robots in the powerhouse, apparently left there by the thoughtful Martian race to prevent entrance to the mysteriously guarded subway station via this route. What was in that station that required so much privacy? Stanton wondered. Something so deadly dangerous that the advanced science of the Martians could not cope with it, but was forced to resort to quarantining the spot where it showed itself? Stanton didn't know the answers, but he was very quiet as a hidden upsurge of memory strove to assert itself. Something that had been in the bobbin-books ... 'The Under-Eaters.' That was it. Had they anything to do with this robot *cordon sanitaire*?

The robots had not noticed them, for which all three were duly grateful. Ogden nudged the nearest to him – it happened to be Annamarie – and thrust out a bony finger. 'Is *that* what the Mars-Tube looks like from inside?' he hissed piercingly.

As their eyes became acclimated to the gloom – they dared use no lights – the others made out the lines of a series of hoops stretching out into blackness on either side ahead of them. No lights anywhere along the chain of rings; no sound coming from it.

'Maybe it's a deserted switch line, one that was abandoned.

That's the way the Tube ought to look, all right, only with cars going along it,' Stanton muttered.

'Hush!' it was Annamarie. 'Would that be a car coming – from the left, way down?'

Nothing was visible, but there was the faintest of sighing sounds. As though an elevator car, cut loose from its cable, were dropping down its shaft far off there in the distance. 'It sounds like a car,' Stanton conceded. 'What do you think, Og – Hey! Where's Josey?'

'He brushed me, going toward the Tube. Yes – there he is! See him? Bending over between those hoops!'

'We've got to get him out of there! Josey!' Stanton cried, forgetting about the robots in the light of this new danger. 'Josey! Get out of the Tube! There's a train coming!'

The dimly visible figure of the Roëntgenologist straightened and turned towards the others querulously. Then as the significance of that rapidly mounting *hiss-s-s-s* became clear to him, he leaped out of the tube, with a vast alacrity. A split second later the hiss had deepened to a high drone, and the bulk of a car shot past them, travelling eerily without visible support, clinging to and being pushed by the intangible fields of force that emanated from the metal hoops of the Tube.

Stanton reached Josey's form in a single bound. 'What were you trying to do, imbecile?' he grated. 'Make an early widow of your prospective fiancée?'

Josey shook off Stanton's grasp with dignity. 'I was merely trying to establish that that string of hoops was the Mars-Tube, by seeing if the power-leads were connected with the rings. It – uh, it was the Tube; that much is proven,' he ended somewhat lamely.

'Brilliant man!' Stanton started to snarl, but Annamarie's voice halted him. It was a very small voice.

'You loud-mouths have been very successful in attracting the attention of those animated pile-drivers,' she whispered with the very faintest of breaths. 'If you will keep your lips zipped for the next little while maybe the robot that's staring at us over the rim of the pit will think we're turbo-generators or something and go away. Maybe!'

Josey swivelled his head up and gasped. 'It's there – it's coming down!' he cried. 'Let's leave here!'

The three backed away toward the tube, slowly, watching the efforts of the machine-thing to descend the precipitous wall. It was having difficulties, and the three were beginning to feel a bit better, when—

Annamarie, turning her head to watch where she was going, saw and heard the cavalcade that was bearing down on them at the same time and screamed shrilly. 'Good Lord – the cavalry!' she yelled. 'Get out your guns!'

A string of a dozen huge, spider-shaped robots of a totally new design were charging down at them, running swiftly along the sides of the rings of the Tube, through the tunnel. They carried no weapons, but the three soon saw why – from the ugly snouts of the egg-shaped bodies of the creatures protruded a black cone. A blinding flash came from the cone of the first of the new arrivals; the aim was bad, for overhead a section of the cement roof flared ghastly white and commenced to drop.

Annamarie had her useless paralyzer out and firing before she realized its uselessness against metal beings with no nervous system to paralyze. She hurled it at the nearest of the new robots in a highly futile gesture of rage.

But the two men had their more potent weapons out and firing, and were taking a toll of the spider-like monstrosities. Three or four of them were down, partially blocking the path of the oncoming others; another was missing all its metal legs along one side of its body, and two of the remainder showed evidence of the accuracy of the Earthmen's fire.

But the odds were still extreme, and the built-it blasters of the robots were coming uncomfortably close.

Stanton saw that, and shifted his tactics. Holstering his heavy blaster, he grabbed Annamarie and shoved her into the

Mars-Tube, crying to Josey to follow. Josey came slowly after them, turning to fire again and again at the robots, but with little effect. A quick look at the charge-dial on the butt of his heat-gun showed why; the power was almost exhausted.

He shouted as much to Stanton. 'I figured that would be happening – now we run!' Stanton cried back, and the three sped along the Mars-Tube, leaping the hoops as they came to them.

'What a time for a hurdle race!' gasped Annamarie, bounding over the rings, which were raised about a foot from the ground. 'You'd think we would have known better than to investigate things that're supposed to be private.'

'Save your breath for running,' panted Josey. 'Are they following us in here?'

Stanton swivelled his head to look, and a startled cry escaped him. 'They're following us – but look!'

The other two slowed, then stopped running altogether and stared in wonder. One of the robots had charged into the Mars-Tube – and had been levitated! He was swinging gently in the air, the long metal legs squirming fiercely, but not touching anything.'

'How —?'

'They're metal!' Annamarie cried. 'Don't you see – they're metal, and the hoops are charged. They must have some of the same metal as the Tube cars are made of in their construction – the force of the hoops acts on them, too!'

That seemed to be the explanation. . . . 'Then we're safe!' gasped Josey, staggering about, looking for a place to sit.

'Not by a long shot! Get moving again!' And Stanton set the example.

'You mean because they can still shoot at us?' Josey cried, following Stanton's dog-trot nonetheless. 'But they can't aim the guns – they seem to be built in, only capable of shooting directly forward.'

'Very true,' gritted Stanton. 'But have you forgotten that this subway is in use? According to my calculations, there

should be another car along in about thirty seconds or less –
and please notice, there isn't any by-path anymore. It stopped
back a couple of hundred feet. If we get caught here by a car,
we get mashed. So – unless you want to go back and sign an
armistice with the robots? I thought not – so we better keep
going. Fast!'

The three were lucky – very lucky. For just when it seemed
certain that they would have to run on and on until the bullet-
fast car overtook them, or go back and face the potent weapons
of the guard robots, a narrow crevice appeared in the side of
the tunnel-wall. The three bolted into it and slumped to the
ground.

CRASH!

'What was that?' cried Annamarie.

'That,' said Josey slowly, 'was what happens to a robot
when the fast express comes by. Just thank God it wasn't us.'

Stanton poked his head gingerly into the Mars-Tube and
stared down. 'Say,' he muttered wonderingly, 'when we wreck
something we do it good. We've ripped out a whole section of
the hoops – by proxy, of course. When the car hit the robot
they were both smashed to atoms, and the pieces knocked out
half a dozen of the suspension rings. I would say, offhand, that
this line has run its last train.'

'Where do you suppose this crevice leads?' asked Annamarie, forgetting the damage that couldn't be undone.

'I don't know. The station ought to be around here some-
where – we were running toward it. Maybe this will lead us
into the station if we follow it. If it doesn't, maybe we can drill
a tunnel from here to the station with my blaster.'

Drilling wasn't necessary. A few feet in, the scarcely pass-
able crevice widened into a broad fissure, through which a
faint light was visible. Exploration revealed that the faint light
came from a wall-chart showing the positions and destinations
of the trains. The chart was displaying the symbol of a Zeta
train – the train that would never arrive.

'Very practical people, we are,' Annamarie remarked with irony. 'We didn't think to bring lights.'

'We never needed them anywhere else on the planet – we can't be blamed too much. Anyway, the code-panel gives us a little light.'

By the steady, dim red glow cast by the code-panel, the three could see the anteroom fairly clearly. It was disappointing. For all they could tell, there was no difference between this and any other station on the whole planet. But why all the secrecy? The dead Martians surely had a reason for leaving the guard-robots so thick and furious. But what was it?

Stanton pressed an ear to the wall of the anteroom. 'Listen!' he snapped. 'Do you hear —?'

'Yes,' said the girl at length. 'Scuffling noises – a sort of gurgling too, like running water passing through pipes.'

'Look there!' wailed Josey.

'Where?' asked the archaeologist naturally. The dark was impenetrable. Or was it? There was a faint glimmer of light, not a reflection from the code-panel, that shone through a continuation of the fissure. It came, not from a single source of light, but from several, eight or ten at least. The lights were bobbing up and down. 'I'd swear they were walking!' marvelled Ray.

'Ray,' shrieked the girl faintly. As the lights grew nearer, she could see what they were – pulsing domes of a purplish glow that ebbed and flowed in tides of dull light. The light seemed to shine from behind a sort of membrane, and the outer surfaces of the membrane were marked off with faces – terrible, savage faces, with carnivorous teeth projecting from mouths that were like ragged slashes edged in writhing red.

'Ray!' Annamarie cried again. 'Those lights – they're the luminous heads of living creatures!'

'God help us – you're right!' Stanton whispered. The patterns of what he had read in the bobbin-books began to form a whole in his mind. It all blended in – 'Under-Eaters,' 'Fiends from Below,' 'Raging Glows.' Those weirdly cryptic creatures that were now approaching. And – 'Good Lord!' Stanton ejaculated, feeling squeamishly sick. 'Look at them – they look like human beings!'

It was true. The resemblance was not great, but the oncoming creatures did have such typically Terrestrial features as hairless bodies, protruding noses, small ears, and so forth, and did not have the unmistakable hour-glass silhouette of the true Martians.

'Maybe that's why the Martians feared and distrusted the first Earthmen they saw. They thought we were related to these – things!' Stanton said thoughtfully.

'Mooning over it won't help us now,' snapped Annamarie. 'What do we do to get away from them? They make me nervous!'

'We don't do anything to get away. What could we do? There's no place to go. We'll have to fight – get out your guns!'

'Guns!' sneered Josey. 'What guns? Mine's practically empty, and Annamarie threw hers away!'

Stanton didn't answer, but looked as though a cannon-shell had struck him amidships. Grimly he drew out his blaster. 'Then this one will have to do all of us,' was all he said. 'If only these accursed blasters weren't so unmanageable – there's at least an even chance that a bad shot will bring the roof down on us. Oh, well – I forgot to mention,' he added casually, 'that, according to the records, the reason that the true Martians didn't like these things was that they had the habit of *eating* their victims. Bearing that in mind, I trust you will not mind my chancing a sudden and unanimous burial for us all.' He drew the blaster and carefully aimed it at the first of the oncoming group. He was already squeezing the trigger when Josey grabbed his arm. 'Hold on, Ray!' Josey whispered. 'Look what's coming.'

The light-headed ones had stopped their inexorable trek toward the Terrestrials. They had bunched fearfully a few yards within the fissure, staring beyond the three humans, into the Mars-Tube.

Three of the spider-robots, the Tube-tenders, were there. Evidently the destruction of one of their number, and the consequent demolition of several of the hoops, had short-circuited this section of the track so that they could enter it and walk along without fear.

There was a deadly silence that lasted for a matter of seconds. The three from Earth cowered as silently as possible where they were, desirous of attracting absolutely no attention from either side. Then – Armageddon!

The three robots charged in, abruptly, lancing straight for the luminous-topped bipeds in the crevasse. Their metal legs stamped death at the relatively impotent organic creatures, trampling their bodies until they died. But the cave-dwellers had their methods of fighting, too; each of them carried some sort of instrument, hard and heavy-ended, with which they wreaked havoc on the more delicate parts of the robots.

More and more 'Raging Glows' appeared from the crevasse, and it seemed that the three robots, heavily outnumbered, would go down to a hard-fought but inevitable 'death' – if that word could be applied to a thing whose only life was electromagnetic. Already there were more than a score of the strange bipeds in the cavern, and destruction of the metal creatures seemed imminent.

'Why don't the idiotic things use their guns?' Annamarie shuddered.

'Same reason I didn't – the whole roof might come down. Don't worry – they're doing all right. Here come some more of them.'

True enough. From the Mars-Tube emerged a running bunch of the robots – ten or more of them. The slaughter was horrible – a carnage made even more unpleasant by the fact that the dimness of the cavern concealed most of the details. The fight was in comparative silence, broken only by the faint metallic clattering of the workings of the robots, and an occasional thin squeal from a crushed biped. The cave-dwellers seemed to have no vocal organs.

The robots were doing well enough even without guns. Their method was simply to trample and bash the internal organs of their opponents until the opponent had died. Then they would kick the pulped corpse out of the way and proceed to the next.

The 'Hot-Heads' had had enough. They broke and ran back down the tunnel from which they had come. The metal feet of the robots clattered on the rubble of the tunnel-floor as they pursued them at maximum speed. It took only seconds for the whole of the ghastly running fight to have traveled so far from the humans as to be out of sight and hearing. The only remnants to show it had ever existed were the mangled corpses of the cave-dwellers, and one or two wrecked robots.

Stanton peered after the battle to make sure it was gone. Then, mopping his brow, he slumped to a sitting position and emitted a vast 'Whew!' of relief. 'I have seldom been so sure I was about to become dead,' he said pensively. 'Divide and rule is what I always say – let your enemies fight it out among themselves. Well, what do we do now? My curiosity is sated – let's go back.'

'That,' said the girl sternly, 'is the thing we are most certainly not going to do. If we've come this far we can go a little farther. Let's go on down this tunnel and see what's there. It seems to branch off farther down; we can take the other route from that of the robots.'

Josey sighed. 'Oh, well,' he murmured resignedly. 'Always game, that's me. Let's travel.'

'It's darker than I ever thought darkness could be, Ray,' Annamarie said tautly. 'And I just thought of something. How do we know *which* is the other route – the one the robots didn't take?'

'A typical question,' snarled Stanton. 'So you get a typical answer: I don't know. Or, to phrase it differently, we just have to put ourselves in the robots' place. If you were a robot, where would you go?'

'Home,' Ogden answered immediately. 'Home and to bed. But these robots took the tunnel we're in. So let's turn back and take the other one.'

'How do you know?'

'Observation and deduction. I observed that I am standing in something warm and squishy, and I deduced that it is the corpse of a recent light-head.'

'No point in taking the other tunnel, though,' Annamarie's voice floated back. She had advanced a few steps and was hugging the tunnel wall. 'There's an entrance to another tunnel here, and it slopes back the way we came. I'd say, offhand, that the other tunnel is just an alternate route.'

'Noise,' said Stanton. 'Listen.'

There was a scrabbling, chittering, quite indescribable sound, and then another one. Suddenly terrific squalling noises broke the underground silence and the three ducked as they sensed something swooping down on them and gliding over their heads along the tunnel.

'What was that?' yelped Josey.

'A cat-fight, I think,' said Stanton. 'I could hear two distinct sets of vocables, and there were sounds of battle. Those things could fly, glide or jump – probably jump. I think they were a specialized form of tunnel life adapted to living, breeding, and fighting in a universe that was long, dark, and narrow. Highly specialized.'

Annamarie giggled hysterically. 'Like the bread-and-butterfly that lived on weak tea with cream in it.'

'Something like,' Stanton agreed.

Hand in hand, they groped their way on through the utter blackness. Suddenly there was a grunt from Josey, on the extreme right. 'Hold it,' he cried, withdrawing his hand to finger his damaged nose. 'The tunnel seems to end here.'

'Not end,' said Annamarie. 'Just turns to the left. And take a look at what's there!'

The men swerved and stared. For a second no one spoke; the sudden new vista was too compelling for speech.

'Ray!' finally gasped the girl. 'It's incredible! It's *incredible!*'

There wasn't a sound from the two men at her sides. They had rounded the final bend in the long tunnel and come out into the flood of light they had seen. The momentary brilliance staggered them and swung glowing spots before their eyes.

Then, as the effects of persistence of vision faded, they saw what the vista actually was. It was a great cavern, the hugest they'd ever seen on either planet – and by tremendous odds the most magnificent.

The walls were not of rock, it seemed, but of slabs of liquid fire – liquid fire which, their stunned eyes soon saw, was a natural inlay of incredible winking gems.

Opulence was the rule of this drusy cave. Not even so base a metal as silver could be seen here; gold was the basest available. Platinum, iridium, little pools of shimmering mercury dotted the jewel-studded floor of the place. Stalactites and stalagmites were purest rock-crystal.

Flames seemed to glow from behind the walls colored by the emerald, ruby, diamond, and topaz. 'How can such a formation occur in nature?' Annamarie whispered. No one answered.

' "There are more things in heaven and under it —" ' raptly misquoted Josey. Then, with a start, 'What act's that from?'

It seemed to bring the others to. 'Dunno,' chorused the archaeologist and the girl. Then, the glaze slowly vanishing from their eyes, they looked at each other.

'Well,' breathed the girl.

In an abstracted voice, as though the vision of the jewels had never been seen, the girl asked, 'How do you suppose the place is lighted?'

'Radioactivity,' said Josey tersely. There seemed to be a tacit agreement – if one did not mention the gems neither would the others. 'Radioactive minerals and maybe plants. All this is natural formation. Weird, of course, but here it is.'

There was a feeble, piping sound in the cavern.

'Can this place harbor life?' asked Stanton in academic tones.

'Of course,' said Josey, 'any place can.' The thin, shrill piping was a little louder, strangely distorted by echoes.

'Listen,' said the girl urgently. 'Do you hear what I hear?'

'Of course not,' cried Stanton worriedly. 'It's just my – I mean our imagination. I can't be hearing what I think I'm hearing.'

Josey had pricked his ears up. 'Calm down, both of you,' he whispered. 'If you two are crazy – so am I. That noise is something – somebody – singing Gilbert and Sullivan. "A Wand'ring Minstrel, I", I believe the tune is.'

'Yes,' said Annamarie hysterically. 'I always liked that number.' Then she reeled back into Stanton's arms, sobbing hysterically.

'Slap her,' said Josey, and Stanton did, her head rolling loosely under the blows. She looked up at him.

'I'm sorry,' she said, the tears still on her cheeks.

'I'm sorry, too,' echoed a voice, thin, reedy, and old; 'and I suppose you're sorry. Put down your guns. Drop them. Put up your hands. Raise them. I really am sorry. After all, I don't *want* to kill you.'

IV

Marshall Ellenbogan

They turned and dropped their guns almost immediately, Stanton shrugging off the heavy power-pack harness of his blaster as Josey cast down his useless heat-pistol. The creature before them was what one would expect as a natural complement to this cavern. He was weird, pixyish, dressed in fantastic points and tatters, stooped, wrinkled, whiskered, and palely luminous. *Induced radioactivity*, Stanton thought.

'Hee,' he giggled. 'Things!'

'We're men,' said Josey soberly. 'Men like – like you.' He shuddered.

'Lord,' marvelled the pixy to himself, his gun not swerving an inch. 'What won't they think of next! Now, now, you efts – you're addressing no puling creature of the deep. I'm a man and proud of it. Don't palter with me. You shall die and be reborn again – eventually, no doubt. I'm no agnostic, efts. Here in this cavern I have seen – oh the things I have seen.' His face was rapturous with holy bliss.

'Who are you?' asked Annamarie.

The pixy started at her, then turned to Josey with a questioning look. 'Is your friend all right?' the pixy whispered confidentially. 'Seems rather effeminate to me.'

'Never mind,' the girl said hastily. 'What's your name?'

'Marshall Ellenbogan,' said the pixy surprisingly. 'Second Lieutenant in the United States Navy. But,' he snickered, 'I suspect my commission's expired.'

'If you're Ellenbogan,' said Stanton, 'then you must be a survivor from the first Mars expedition. The one that started the war.'

'Exactly,' said the creature. He straightened himself with a sort of somber dignity. 'You can't know,' he groaned, you never could know what we went through. Landed in a desert. Then we trekked for civilization – all of us, except three kids that we left in the ship. I've often wondered what happened to them.' He laughed. 'Civilization! Cold-blooded killers who tracked us down like vermin. Killed Kelly, Keogh. Moley. Jumped on us and killed us – like that.' He made a futile attempt to snap his fingers. 'But not me – not Ellenbogan – I ducked behind a rock and they fired on the rock and rock and me both fell into a cavern. I've wandered – Lord! how I've wandered. How long ago was it, efts?'

The lucid interval heartened the explorers. 'Fifty years, Ellenbogan,' said Josey. 'What did you live on all that time?'

'Moss-fruits from the big white trees. Meat now and then,

eft, when I could shoot one of your light-headed brothers.' He leered. 'But I won't eat you. I haven't tasted meat for so long now ... Fifty years. That makes me seventy years old. You efts never live for more than three or four years, you don't know how long seventy years can be.'

'We aren't efts,' snapped Stanton. 'We're human beings same as you. I swear we are! And we want to take you back to Earth where you can get rid of that poison you've been soaking into your system! Nobody can live in a radium-impregnated cave for fifty years and still be healthy. Ellenbogan, for God's sake be reasonable!'

The gun did not fall nor waver. The ancient creature regarded them shrewdly, his head cocked to one side. 'Tell me what happened,' he said at length.

'There was a war,' said the girl. 'It was about you and the rest of the expedition that had been killed. When you didn't come back, the Earth governments sent another expedition – armed this time, because the kids you left in the ship managed to raise Earth for a short time when they were attacked, and they told the whole story. The second expedition landed, and – well, it's not very clear. We only have the ship's log to go by, but it seems to have been about the same with them. Then the Earth governments raised a whole fleet of rocket-ships, with everything in the way of guns and ray-projectors they could hold installed. And the Martians broke down the atomic-power process from one of the Earth ships they'd captured, and *they* built a fleet. And there was a war, the first interplanetary war in history. For neither side ever took prisoners. There's some evidence that the Martians realized they'd made a mistake at the beginning after the war had been going only about three years, but by that time it was too late to stop. And it went on for fifty years, with rocket-ships getting bigger and faster and better, and new weapons being developed ... Until finally we developed a mind-disease that wiped out the entire Martian race in half a year. They were telepathic, you know, and that helped spread the disease.'

'Good for them,' snarled the elder. 'Good for the treacherous, devilish, double-dealing rats . . . And what are you people doing here now?'

'We're an exploring party, sent by the new all-Earth confederation to examine the ruins and salvage what we can of their knowledge. We came on you here quite by accident. We haven't got any evil intentions. We just want to take you back to your own world. You'll be a hero there. Thousands will cheer you – millions. Ellenbogan, put down your gun. Look – we put ours down!'

'Hah!' snarled the pixy, retreating a pace. 'You had me going for a minute. But not any more!' With a loud click, the pixy thumbed the safety catch of his decades-old blaster. He reached back to the power-pack he wore across his back, which supplied energy for the weapon, and spun the wheel to maximum output. The power-pack was studded with rubies which, evidently, he had hacked with diamonds into something resembling finished, faceted stones.

'Wait a minute, Ellenbogan,' Stanton said desperately. 'You're the king of these parts, aren't you? Don't you want to keep us for subjects?'

'Monarch of all I survey, eft. Alone and undisputed.' His brow wrinkled. 'Yes, eft,' he sighed, 'you are right. You efts are growing cleverer and cleverer – you begin almost to understand how I feel. Sometimes a king is lonely – sometimes I long for companionship – on a properly deferential plane, of course. Even you efts I would accept as my friends if I did not know that you wanted no more than my blood. I can never be the friend of an eft. Prepare to die.'

Josey snapped: 'Are you going to kill the girl, too?'

'Girl?' cried the pixy in amazement. 'What girl?' His eyes drifted to Annamarie Hudgins. 'Bless me,' he cried, his eyes bulging. 'Why, so he is! I mean, she is! That would explain it, of course, wouldn't it?'

'Of course,' said Stanton. 'But you're not going to kill her, are you?'

'If she were an eft,' mused the pixy, 'I certainly would. But I'm beginning to doubt that she is. In fact, you're probably all almost as human as I am. However —' He mistily surveyed her.

'Girl,' he asked dreamily, 'do you want to be a queen?'

'Yes, sir,' said Annamarie, preventing a shudder. 'Nothing would give me more pleasure.'

'So be it,' said the ancient, with great decision. 'So be it. The ceremony of coronation can wait till later, but you are now ex officio my consort.'

'That is splendid,' cried Annamarie, 'simply splendid.' She essayed a chuckle of pleasure, but which turned out to be a dismal choking sound. 'You've — you've made me positively the happiest woman under Mars.'

She walked stiffly over to the walking monument commemorating what had once been a man, and kissed him gingerly on the forehead. The pixy's seamed face glowed for more reasons than the induced radioactivity as Stanton stared in horror.

'The first lesson of a queen is obedience,' said the pixy fondly, 'so please sit there and do not address a word to these unfortunate former friends of yours. They are about to die.'

'Oh,' pouted Annamarie. 'You are cruel, Ellenbogan.'

He turned anxiously, though keeping the hair-trigger weapon full on the two men. 'What troubles you, sweet?' he demanded. 'You have but to ask and it shall be granted. We are lenient to our consort.'

The royal 'we' already thought Stanton. He wondered if the ancient would be in the market for a coat of arms. Three years of freehand drawing in his high school in Cleveland had struck Stanton as a dead waste up till now; suddenly it seemed that it might save his life.

'How,' Annamarie was complaining, 'can I be a real queen without any subjects?'

The pixy was immediately suspicious, but the girl looked at him so blandly that his ruffles settled down. He scratched his head with the hand that did not hold the blaster. 'True,' he admitted. 'I hadn't thought of that. Very well, you may have a subject. One subject.'

'I think two would be much nicer,' Annamarie said a bit worriedly, though she retained the smile.

'One!'

'Please – two?'

'One! One is enough. Which of these two shall I kill?'

Now was the time to start the sales-talk about the coat-of-arms, thought Stanton. But he was halted in mid-thought, the words informed, by Annamarie's astonishing actions. Puckering her brow so very daintily, she stepped over to the pixy and slipped an arm about his waist. 'It's hard to decide,' she remarked languidly staring from one to the other, still with her arm about the pixy. 'But I think —

'Yes. I think – kill *that* one.' And she pointed at Stanton.

Stanton didn't stop to think about what a blaster could do to a promising career as artist by appointment to Mars' only monarch. He jumped – lancing straight as a string in the weak Martian gravity, directly at the figure of the ancient. He struck and bowled him over. Josey, acting a second later, landed on top of him, the two piled on to the pixy's slight figure. Annamarie, wearing a twisted smile, stepped aside and watched quite calmly.

Oddly enough, the pixy had not fired the blaster.

After a second, Stanton's voice came smotheredly from the wriggling trio. He was addressing Josey. 'Get up, you oaf,' he said. 'I think the old guy is dead.'

Josey clambered to his feet, then knelt again to examine Ellenbogan. 'Heart-failure, I guess,' he said briefly. 'He was pretty old.'

Stanton was gently prodding a swelling eye. 'Your fault, idiot,' he glared at Josey. 'I doubt that one of your roundhouse swings touched Ellenbogan. And as for you, friend,' he sneered, turning to Annamarie, 'you have my most heartfelt sympathies. Not for worlds would I have made you a widow so soon, I apologize,' and he bowed low, recovering himself with some difficulty.

'Did it ever occur to you,' Annamarie said tautly – Stanton was astounded as he noticed she was trembling with a nervous reaction – 'did it ever occur to you that maybe you owe me something? Because if I hadn't disconnected his blaster from the power-pack, you would be —'

Stanton gaped as she turned aside to hide a flood of sudden tears, which prevented her from completing the sentence. He dropped to one knee and ungently turned over the old man's body. Right enough – the lead between power-pack and gun was dangling loose, jerked from its socket. He rose again and, staring at her shaking figure, stepped unsteadily toward her.

Josey, watching them with scientific impersonality, upcurled a lip in the beginnings of a sneer. Then suddenly the sneer died in birth, and was replaced by a broad smile. 'I've seen it coming for some time,' more loudly than was necessary, 'and I want to be the first to congratulate you. I hope you'll be very happy,' he said ...

A few hours later, they stared back at the heap of earth under which was the body of the late Second Lieutenant Ellenbogan, U.S.N., and quietly made their way toward the walls of the cavern. Choosing a different tunnel-mouth for the attempt, they began the long trek to the surface. Though at first Stanton and Annamarie walked hand-in-hand, it was soon arm-in-arm, then with arms around each other's waists, while Josey trailed sardonically behind.

The Quaker Cannon

I

Lieutenant John Kramer did crossword puzzles during at least eighty per cent of his waking hours. His cubicle in Bachelor Officers Quarters was untidy; one wall was stacked solid with newspapers and magazines to which he subscribed for their puzzle pages. He meant, from week to week, to clean them out but somehow never found time. The ern, or erne, a sea eagle, soared vertically through his days and by night the ai, a three-toed sloth, crept horizontally. In edes, or Dutch communes, dyers retted ecru, quaffing ades by the tun and thought was postponed.

John Kramer was in disgrace and, at thirty-eight, well on his way to becoming the oldest first lieutenant in the North American (and Allied) Army. He had been captured in '82 as an aftermath of the confused fighting around Tsingtao. A few exquisitely unpleasant months passed and he then delivered three TV lectures for the yutes. In them he announced his total conversion to Neo-Utilitarianism, denounced the North American (and Allied) military command as a loathesome pack of war-waging, anti-utilitarian mad dogs, and personally admitted the waging of viral warfare against the United Utilitarian Republics.

The yutes, or Utilitarians, had been faithful to their principles. They had wanted Kramer only for what he could do for them, not for his own sweet self, and when they had got the juice out of him they exchanged him. In '83 he came out of his fog at Fort Bradley, Utah, to find himself being court-martialed.

He was found guilty as charged, and sentenced to a reprimand. The lightness of the sentence was something to be a little proud of, if not very much. It stood as a grudging tribute to the months he had held out against involutional melancholia in the yute Blank Tanks. For exchanged PW's, the severity of their court-martial was in inverse proportion to the duration of their ordeal in Utilitarian hands. Soldiers who caved in after a couple of days of sense-starvation could look forward only to a firing squad. Presumably a returned soldier dogged (or rigid) enough to be driven into hopeless insanity without cooperating would have been honorably acquitted by his court, but such a case had not yet come up.

Kramer's 'reprimand' was not the face-to-face bawling-out suggested to a civilian by the word. It was a short letter with numbered paragraphs which said (1) you are reprimanded, (2) a copy of this reprimand will be punched on your profile card. This tagged him forever as a foulball, destined to spend the rest of his military life shuffling from one dreary assignment to another, without hope of promotion or reward.

He no longer cared. Or thought he did not; which came to the same thing.

He was not liked in the Officers Club. He was bad company. Young officers passing through Bradley on their way to glory might ask him, 'What's it *really* like in a Blank Tank, Kramer?' But beyond answering, 'You go nuts,' what was there to talk about? Also he did not drink, because when he drank he went on to become drunk, and if he became drunk he would cry.

So he did a crossword puzzle in bed before breakfast, dressed, went to his office, signed papers, did puzzles until lunch, and so on until the last one in bed at night. Nominally he was Commanding Officer of the 561st Provisional Reception Battalion. Actually he was (with a few military overtones) the straw boss of a gang of clerks in uniform who saw to the arrival, bedding, feeding, equipping, inoculation and transfer to a training unit of one thousand scared kids per week.

On a drizzle-swept afternoon in the spring of '85 Kramer was sounding one of those military overtones. It was his appointed day for a 'surprise' inspection of Company D of his battalion. Impeccable in dress blues, he was supposed to descend like a

thunderbolt on this company or that, catching them all un-
aware, striding arrogantly down the barracks aisle between
bunks, white-gloved and eagle-eyed for dust, maddened at the
sight of disarray, vengeful against such contraband as playing
cards or light reading matter. Kramer knew, quite well, that
one of his orderly room clerks always telephoned the doomed
company to warn that he was on his way. He did not particularly mind it. What he minded was unfair definitions of
key words, and ridiculously variant spellings.

The permanent-party sergeant of D Company bawled
'Tench*hun*!' when Kramer snapped the door open and stepped crisply into the barracks. Kramer froze his face into its
approved expression of controlled annoyance and opened his
mouth to give the non-com his orders. But the sergeant had
miscalculated. One of the scared kids was still frantically
mopping the aisle.

Kramer halted. The kid spun around in horror, made some
kind of attempt to present arms with the mop and failed. The
mop shot from his soapy hands like a slung baseball bat, and
its soggy gray head schlooped against the lieutenant's dress-
blue chest.

The kid turned white and seemed about to faint on the
damp board floor. The other kids waited to see him destroyed.

Kramer was mildly irritated. 'At ease,' he said. 'Pick up
that mop. Sergeant, confound it, next time they buzz you from
the orderly room don't cut it so close.'

The kids sighed perceptibly and glanced covertly at each
other in the big bare room, beginning to suspect it might not
be too bad after all. Lieutenant Kramer then resumed the expression of a nettled bird of prey and strode down the aisle.
Long ago he had worked out a 'random' selection of bunks for
special attention and now followed it through habit. If he had
thought about it any more, he would have supposed that it was
still spy-proof; but every non-com in his cadre had long since
discovered that Kramer stopped at either every second bunk
on the right and every third on the left, or every third bunk on

the right and every second on the left – depending on whether the day of the month was odd or even. This would not have worried Kramer if he had known it; but he never even noticed that the men beside the bunks he stopped at were always the best-shaved, best-policed and healthiest looking in each barracks.

Regardless, he delivered a certain quota of meaningless demerits which were gravely recorded by the sergeant. Of blue-eyed men on the left and brown-eyed men on the right (this, at least, had not been penetrated by the non-coms) he went on to ask their names and home towns. Before discovering crossword puzzles he had memorized atlases, so he had something to say about every home town he had yet encountered. In this respect at least he considered himself an above-average officer, and indeed he was.

It wasn't the Old Army, not by a long shot, but when the draft age went down to 15 some of the Old Army's little ways had to go. One experimental reception station in Virginia was trying out a Barracks Mother system. Kramer, thankful for small favors, was glad they hadn't put him on that project. Even here he was expected, at the end of the inspection, to call the 'men' around him and ask if anything was bothering them. Something always was. Some gangling kid would scare up the nerve to ask, gee, lieutenant, I know what the Morale Officer said, but exactly *why* didn't we ever use the megaton-head missiles, and another would want to know how come Lunar Base was such a washout, tactically speaking, sir. And then he would have to rehearse the dry 'recommended discussion themes' from the briefing books; and then, finally, one of them, nudged on by others, would pipe up, 'Lieutenant, what's it *like* in the Blank Tanks?' And he would know that already, forty-eight hours after induction, the kids all knew about what Lieutenant John Kramer had done.

But today he was spared. When he was halfway through the rigmarole the barracks phone rang and the sergeant apologetically answered it.

He returned from his office-cubicle on the double, looking vaguely frightened. 'Compliments of General Grote's secretary, sir, and will you please report to him at G-1 as soon as possible.'

'Thank you, sergeant. Step outside with me a moment.' Out on the duckboard walk, with the drizzle trickling down his neck, he asked: 'Sergeant, who is General Grote?'

'Never heard of him, sir.'

Neither had Lieutenant Kramer.

He hurried to Bachelor Officers Quarters to change his sullied blue jacket, not even pausing to glance at the puzzle page of the *Times*, which had arrived while he was at 'work.' Generals were special. He hurried out again into the drizzle.

Around him and unnoticed were the artifacts of an army base at war. Sky-eye search radars popped from their silos to scan the horizons for a moment and then retreat, the burden of search taken up by the next in line. Helicopter sentries on guard duty prowled the barbed-wire perimeter of the camp. Fort Bradley was not all reception center. Above-ground were the barracks, warehouses and rail and highway termini for processing recruits – ninety thousand men and all their goods – but they were only the skin over the fort itself. They were, as the scared kids told each other in the dayrooms, naked to the air. If the yutes ever *did* spring a megaton attack, they would become a thin coating of charcoal on the parade ground, but they would not affect the operation of the *real* Fort Bradley a bit.

The *real* Fort Bradley was a hardened installation beneath meters of reinforced concrete, some miles of rambling warrens that held the North American (and Allied) Army's G-1. It's business was people: the past, present and future of every soul in the Army.

G-1 decided that a fifteen-year-old in Duluth was unlikely to succeed in civilian schools and drafted him. G-1 punched his Army tests and civilian records on cards, consulted its card-punched tables of military requirements and assigned him, perhaps, to Machinist Training rather than Telemetering School. G-1 yanked a platoon leader halfway around the world from Formosa and handed him a commando for a raid on the yutes' Polar Station Seven. G-1 put foulball Kramer at the 'head' of the 561st PRB. G-1 promoted and allocated and staffed and rewarded and punished.

Foulball Kramer approached the guardbox at the elevators to the warrens and instinctively squared his shoulders and smoothed his tie.

General Grote, he thought. He hadn't *seen* a general officer since he'd been commissioned. Not close up. Colonels and majors had court-martialed him. He didn't know who Grote was, whether he had one star or six, whether he was Assignment, Qualifications, Training, Evaluation, Psychological – or Disciplinary.

Military Police looked him over at the elevator head. They read him like a book. Kramer wore his record on his chest and sleeves. Dull gold bars spelled out the overseas months – for his age and arm, the Infantry, not enough. 'Formosa,' said a green ribbon, and 'the storming of the beach' said a small bronze spearpoint on it. A brown ribbon told them 'Chinese Mainland,' and the stars on it meant that he had engaged in three of the five mainland campaigns – presumably Canton, Mukden and Tsingtao, since they were the first. After that, nothing. Especially not the purple ribbon that might indicate a wound serious enough to keep him out of further fighting.

The ribbons, his age and the fact that he was still a first lieutenant were grounds enough for the MPs to despise him. An officer of 38 should be a captain at least. Many were majors and some were colonels. 'You can go down, Lieutenant,' they told the patent foulball, and he went down to the interminable concrete tunnels of G-1.

A display machine considered the name *General Grote* when he typed it on its keyboard, and told him with a map where the general was to be found. It was a longish walk through the tunnels. While he walked past banks of clicking card-sorters and their servants he pondered other information the machine had gratuitously supplied:

GROTE, Lawrence W, Lit Gen, 0-459732, Unassigned

It did not lessen any of Kramer's puzzles. A three-star general, then. He couldn't *possibly* have anything to do with disciplining a lousy first-john. Lieutenant generals ran Army Groups, gigantic ad hoc assemblages of up to a hundred divisions, complete with air forces, missile groups, amphibious assault teams, even carrier and missile-sub forces. The fact of his rank indicated that, whoever he was, he was an immensely able and tenacious person. He had gone through at least a twenty-year threshing of the wheat from the chaff, all up the screening and evaluation boards from second lieutenant to, say, lieutenant colonel, and then the murderous grind of accelerated course at Command and General Staff School, the fanatically rigid selection for the War College, an obstacle course designed not to train the sub-standard up to competence but to keep them out. It was just this side of impossible for a human being to become a lieutenant general. And yet a few human being in every generation did bulldoze their way through that little gap between the impossible and the almost impossible.

And such a man was unassigned?

Kramer found the office at last. A motherly, but sharp-eyed, WAC major told him to go right in.

John Kramer studied his three-star general while going through the ancient rituals of reporting-as-ordered. General Grote was an old man, straight, spare, white-haired, tanned. He wore no overseas bars. On his chest were all the meritorious ribbons his country could bestow, but none of the decorations of the combat soldier. This was explained by a modest sunburst centered over the ribbons. General Grote was, had always been, General Staff Corps. A desk man.

'Sit down, lieutenant,' Grote said, eyeing him casually. 'You've never heard of me, I assume.'

'I'm afraid not, sir.'

'As I expected,' said Grote complacently. 'I'm not a dashing tank commander or one of those flying generals who leads his own raids. I'm one of the people who moves the dashing tank commanders and flying generals around the board like chess pieces. And now, confound it, I'm going to be a dashing combat leader at last. You may smoke if you like.'

Kramer obediently lit up.

'Dan Medway,' said the general, 'wants me to start from scratch, build up a striking force and hit the Asian mainland across the Bering Strait.'

Kramer was horrified twice – first by the reference to The Supreme Commander as 'Dan' and second by the fact that he, a lieutenant, was being told about high strategy.

'Relax,' the general said. 'Why you're here, now. You're going to be my aide.'

Kramer was horrified again. The general grinned.

'Your card popped out of the machinery,' he said, and that was all there was to say about that, 'and so you're going to be a highly privileged character and everybody will detest you. That's the way it is with aides. You'll know everything I know. And vice versa; that's the important part. You'll run errands for me, do investigations, serve as hatchet man, see that my pajamas are pressed without starch and make coffee the way I like it – coarse grind, brought to the boil for just a moment in an old-fashioned coffee pot. Actually what you'll do is what I want you to do from day to day. For these privileges you get to wear a blue fourragère around your left shoulder which marks you as a man not to be trifled with by colonels, brigadiers or MPs. That's the way it is with aides. And, I don't know if you have any outside interests, women or chess or drinking. The machinery didn't mention any. But you'll have to give them up if you do.'

'Yes, sir,' said Kramer. And it seemed wildly possible that

he might never touch pencil to puzzle again. With something
to *do* —

'We're Operation Ripsaw,' said the general. 'So far, that's
me, Margaret out there in the office and you. In addition to
other duties, you'll keep a diary of Ripsaw, by the way, and I
want you to have a summary with you at all times in case I
need it. Now call in Margaret, make a pot of coffee, there's a
little stove thing in the washroom there, and I'll start putting
together my general staff.'

It started as small and as quietly as that.

II

It was a week before Kramer got back to the 561st long
enough to pick up his possessions, and then he left the stacks
of *Timeses* and *Saturday Reviews* where they lay, puzzles and
all. No time. The first person to hate him was Margaret,
the motherly major. For all her rank over him, she was a secretary and he was an aide with a fourragère who had the general's willing ear. She began a policy of non-resistance that
was non-cooperation, too; she would not deliberately obstruct
him, but she would allow him to poke through the files for ten
minutes before volunteering the information that the folder he
wanted was already on the general's desk. This interfered with
the smooth performance of Kramer's duties, and of course the
general spotted it at once.

'It's nothing,' said Kramer when the general called him on
it. 'I don't like to say anything.'

'Go on,' General Grote urged. 'You're not a soldier any
more; you're a rat.'

'I think I can handle it, sir.'

The general motioned silently to the coffee pot and waited
while Kramer fixed him a cup, two sugars, no cream. He said :
'Tell me everything, always. All the dirty rumors about in-
efficiency and favoritism. Your suspicions and hunches. Anybody that gets in your way – or more important, in mine. In

the underworld they shoot stool-pigeons, but here we give them blue cords for their shoulders. Do you understand?'

Kramer did. He did not ask the general to intercede with the motherly major, or transfer her; but he did handle it himself. He discovered it was very easy. He simply threatened to have her sent to Narvik.

With the others it was easier. Margaret had resented him because she was senior in Operation Ripsaw to him, but as the others were sucked in they found him there already. Instead of resentment, their attitude toward him was purely fear.

The next people to hate him were the aides of Grote's general staff because he was a wild card in the deck. The five members of the staff – Chief, Personnel, Intelligence, Plans & Training and Operations – proceeded with their orderly, systematic jobs day by day, building Ripsaw ... until the inevitable moment when Kramer would breeze in with, 'Fine job, but the general suggests —' and the unhorsing of many assumptions, and the undoing of many days' work. That was his job also. He was a bird of ill omen, a coiled snake in fair grass, a hired killer and a professional betrayer of confidences – though it was not long before there were no confidences to betray, except from an occasional young, new officer who hadn't learned his way around, and those not worth betraying. That, as the general had said, was the way it was with aides. Kramer wondered sometimes if he liked what he was doing, or liked himself for doing it. But he never carried the thought through. No time.

Troops completed basic training or were redeployed from rest areas and entrained, emplaned, embussed or embarked for the scattered staging areas of Ripsaw. Great forty-wheeled trucks bore nuclear cannon up the Alcan Highway at a snail's pace. Air groups and missile sections launched on training exercises over Canadian wasteland that closely resembled tundra, with grid maps that bore names like Maina Pylgin and Kamenskoe. Yet these were not Ripsaw, not yet, only the separate tools that Ripsaw would someday pick up and use.

Ripsaw itself moved to Wichita and a base of its own when its headquarters staff swelled to fifteen hundred men and women. Most of them hated Kramer.

It was never perfectly clear to Kramer what his boss had to do with the show. Kramer made his coffee, carried his briefcase, locked and unlocked his files, delivered to him those destructive tales and delivered for him those devastating suggestions, but never understood just why there had to be a Commanding General of Ripsaw.

The time they went to Washington to argue an allocation of 70 rather than 60 armored divisions for Ripsaw, for instance, General Grote just sat, smiled and smoked his pipe. It was his chief of staff, the young and brilliant major general Cartmill, who passionately argued the case before D. Beauregard Medway, though when Grote addressed his superior it was still as 'Dan.' (They did get the 10 extra divisions, of course.)

Back in Wichita, it was Cartmill who toiled around the clock coordinating. A security lid was clamped down early in the game. The fifteen hundred men and women in the Wichita camp stayed in the Wichita camp. Commerce with the outside world, except via coded messages to other elements of Ripsaw, was a capital offense – as three privates learned the hard way. But through those coded channels Cartmill reached out to every area of the North American (and Allied) world. Personnel scoured the globe for human components that might be fitted into Ripsaw. Intelligence gathered information about that tract of Siberia which they were to invade, and the waters they were to cross. Plans & Training slaved at methods of effecting the crossing and invasion efficiently, with the least (or at any rate the optimum least, consistent with requirements of speed, security and so on) losses in men and material. Operations studied and restudied the various ways the crossing and invasion might go right or wrong, and how a good turn of fortune could be exploited, a bad turn minimized. General Cartmill was in constant touch with all of them, his fingers on every cord in the web. So was John Kramer.

Grote ambled about all this with an air of pleased surprise.

Kramer discovered one day that there had been books written about his boss – not best-sellers with titles like 'Bloody Larry' Grote, Sword of Freedom, but thick, gray mimeographed staff documents, in Chinese and Russian, for top-level circulation among yute commanders. He surprised Grote reading one of them – in Chinese.

The general was not embarrassed. 'Just refreshing my memory of what the yutes think I'm like so I can cross them up by doing something different. Listen "Characteristic of this officer's philosophy of attack is varied tactics. Reference his lecture, Lee's 1862 Campaigns, delivered at Fort Leavenworth Command & General Staff School, attached. Opposing commanders should not expect a force under him to do the same —" Hmm. Tsueng, water radical. "– under him to press the advance the same way twice." Now all I have to do is make sure we attack by the book, like Grant instead of Lee, slug it out without any brilliant variations. See how easy it is, John? How's the message center?'

Kramer had been snooping around the message center at Grote's request. It was a matter of feeding out cigarettes and smiles in return for an occasional incautious word or a hint; gumshoe work. The message center was an underground complex of encoders, decoders, transmitters, receivers and switchboards. It was staffed by a Signal Corps WAC battalion in three shifts around the clock. The girls were worked hard – though a battalion should have been enough for the job. Messages went from and to the message center linking the Wichita brain with those 70 divisions training now from Capetown to Manitoba, a carrier task force conducting exercises in the Antarctic, a fleet of landing craft growing every day on the Gulf of California. The average timelag between receipt of messages and delivery to the Wichita personnel at destination was 12.25 minutes. The average number of erroneous transmissions detected per day was three. Both figures General Grote considered intolerable.

'It's Colonel Bucknell that's lousing it up, General. She's trying too hard. No give. Physical training twice a day, for instance, and a very hard policy on excuses. A stern attitude's filtered down from her to the detachments. Everybody's chewing out subordinates to keep themselves covered. The working girls call Bucknell "the monster." Their feeling is the Army's impossible to please, so what the hell.'

'Relieve her.' Grote said amiably. 'Make her mess officer; Ripsaw chow's rotten anyway.' He went back to his Chinese text.

And suddenly it all began to seem as if it really might someday rise and strike out across the Strait. From Lieutenant Kramer's Ripsaw Diary:

At AM staff meeting CG RIPSAW xmitted order CG NAAARMY designating RIPSAW D day 15 May 1986. Gen CARTMILL observed this date allowed 45 days to form troops in final staging areas assuming RIPSAW could be staged in 10 days. CG RIPSAW stated that a 10-day staging seemed feasible. Staff concurred. CG RIPSAW so ordered. At 1357 hours CG NAAARMY concurrence received.

They were on the way.

As the days grew shorter Grote seemed to have less and less to do, and curiously so did Kramer. He had not expected this. He had been aide-de-camp to the general for nearly a year now, and he fretted when he could find no fresh treason to bring to the general's ears. He redoubled his prowling tours of the kitchens, the BOQ, the motor pools, the message center, but not even the guard mounts or the shine on the shoes of the soldiers at Retreat parade was in any way at fault. Kramer could only imagine that he was missing things. It did not occur to him that, as at last they should be, the affairs of Ripsaw had gathered enough speed to keep them straight and clean, until the general called him in one night and ordered him to pack. Grote put on his spectacles and looked over them at Kramer. 'D plus five,' he said, 'assuming all goes well, we're moving this headquarters to Kiska. I want you to take a look-see. Arrange a plane. You can leave tomorrow.'

It was, Kramer realized that night as he undressed, Just Something to Do. Evidently the hard part of his job was at an end. It was now only a question of fighting the battle, and for that the field commanders were much more important than he. For the first time in many months he thought it would be nice to do a crossword puzzle, but instead fell asleep.

It was an hour before leaving the next day that Kramer met Ripsaw's 'cover.'

The 'cover' was another lieutenant general, a bristling and wiry man named Clough, with a brilliant combat record staked out on his chest and sleeves for the world to read. Kramer came in when his buzzer sounded, made coffee for the two generals and was aware that Grote and Clough were old pals and that the Ripsaw general was kidding the pants off his guest.

'You always were a great admirer of Georgie Patton,' Grote teased. 'You should be glad to follow in his footsteps. Your operation will go down in history as big and important as his historic cross-Channel smash into Le Havre.'

Kramer's thoughts were full of himself – he did not much like getting even so close to the yutes as Kiska, where he would be before the sun set that night – but his ears pricked up. He could not remember any cross-Channel smash into Le Havre. By Patton or anybody else.

'Just because I came to visit your show doesn't mean you have to rib me, Larry,' Clough grumbled.

'But it's such a pleasure, Mick.'

Clough opened his eyes wide and looked at Grote. 'I've generaled against Novotny before. If you want to know what I think of him, I'll tell you.'

Pause. Then Grote, gently: 'Take it easy, Mick. Look at

my boy there. See him quivering with curiosity?'

Kramer's back was turned. He hoped his blush would subside before he had to turn around with the coffee. It did not.

'Caught red-faced,' Grote said happily, and winked at the other general. Clough looked stonily back. 'Shall we put him out of his misery, Mick? Shall we fill him in on the big picture?'

'Might as well get it over with.'

'I accept your gracious assent.' Grote waved for Kramer to help himself to coffee and to sit down. Clearly he was unusually cheerful today, Kramer thought. Grote said: . 'Lieutenant Kramer, General Clough is the gun-captain of a Quaker cannon which covers Ripsaw. He looks like a cannon. He acts like a cannon. But he isn't loaded. Like his late idol George Patton at one point in his career, General Clough is the commander of a vast force which exists on paper and radio transmissions alone.'

Clough stirred uneasily, so Grote became more serious. 'We're brain-washing Continental Defense Commissar Novotny by serving up to him his old enemy as the man he'll have to fight. The yute radio intercepts are getting a perfect picture of an assault on Polar Nine being prepared under old Mick here. That's what they'll prepare to counter, of course. Ripsaw will catch them flatfooted.'

Clough stirred again but did not speak.

Grote grinned. 'All right. We *hope*,' he conceded. 'But there's a lot of planning in this thing. Of course, it's a waste of the talent of a rather remarkably able general —' Clough gave him a lifted-eyebrow look – 'but you've got to have a real man at the head of the fake army group or they won't believe it. Anyway, it worked with Patton and the Nazis. Some unkind people have suggested that Patton never did a better piece of work than sitting on his knapsack in England and letting his name be used.'

'All full of beans with a combat command, aren't you?' Clough said sourly. 'Wait'll the shooting starts.'

'Ike never commanded a battalion before the day he invaded North Africa, Mick. He did all right.'

'Ike wasn't up against Novotny,' Clough said heavily. 'I can talk better while I'm eating, Larry. Want to buy me a lunch?'

General Grote nodded. 'Lieutenant, see what you can charm out of Colonel Bucknell for us to eat, will you? We'll have it sent in here, of course, and the best girls she's got to serve it.' Then, unusually, he stood up and looked appraisingly at Kramer.

'Have a nice flight,' he said.

III

Kramer's blue fourragère won him cold handshakes but a seat at the first table in the Hq Officers Mess in Kiska. He didn't have quite enough appetite to appreciate it.

Approaching the island from the air had taken appetite away from him, as the GCA autocontroller rocked the plane in a carefully calculated zigzag in its approach. They were, Kramer discovered, under direct visual observation from any chance-met bird from yute across the Strait until they got below five hundred feet. Sometimes the yutes sent over a flight of birds to knock down a transport. Hence the zigzags.

Captain Mabry, a dark, tall Georgian who had been designated to make the general's aide feel at home, noticed Kramer wasn't eating, pushed his own tray into the center strip and, as it sailed away, stood up. 'Get it off the pad, shall we? Can't keep the Old Man waiting.'

The captain took Kramer through clanging corridors to an elevator and then up to the eyrie. It was only a room. From it the spy-bird missiles – rockets, they were really, but the services like to think of them as having a punch, even though the punch was only a television camera – were controlled. To it the birds returned the pictures their eyes saw.

Brigadier Spiegelhauer shook Kramer's hand. 'Make yourself at home, Lieutenant,' he boomed. He was short and almost skeletally thin, but his voice was enormous. 'Everything satisfactory for the general, I hope?'

'Why, yes, sir. I'm just looking around.'

'Of course,' Spiegelhauer shouted. 'Care to monitor a ride?'

'Yes, sir.' Mabry was looking at him with amusement, Kramer saw. Confound him, what right did *he* have to think Kramer was scared – even if he was? Not a physical fear; he was not insane. But . . . scared.

The service life of a spy-bird over yute territory was something under twenty minutes, by then the homing heads on the ground-to-air birds would have sniffed out its special fragrance and knocked it out. In that twenty-minute period it would see what it could see. Through its eyes the observers in the eyrie would learn just that much more about yute dispositions – so long as it remained in direct line-of-sight to the eyrie, so long as everything in its instrumentation worked, so long as yute jamming did not penetrate its microwave control.

Captain Mabry took Kramer's arm. 'Take 'er off the pad,' Mabry said negligently to the launch officer. He conducted Kramer to a pair of monitors and sat before them.

On both eight-inch screens the officers saw a diamond-sharp scan of the inside of a silo plug. There was no sound. The plug lifted off its lip without a whisper, dividing into two semicircles of steel. A two-inch circle of sky showed. Then, abruptly, the circle widened; the lip irised out and disappeared; the gray surrounded the screen and blanked it out, and then it was bright blue, and a curl of cirrocumulus in one quadrant of the screen.

Metro had promised no cloud over the tactical area, but there was cloud there. Captain Mabry frowned and tapped a tune on the buttons before him; the cirrocumulus disappeared and a line of gray-white appeared at an angle on the screen. 'Horizon,' said Mabry. 'Labble to make you seasick, Lootenant.' He tapped some more and the image righted itself. A faint yellowish stain, not bright against the bright cloud, curved up before them and burst into spidery black smoke.

'Oh, they are *anxious*,' said Mabry, sounding nettled. 'General, weather has busted it again. Cain't see a thing.'

Spiegelhauer bawled angrily, 'I'm going to the weather station,' and stamped out. Kramer knew what he was angry about. It was not the waste of a bird; it was that he had been made to lose face before the general's aide-de-camp. There would be a bad time for the Weather Officer because Kramer had been there that day.

The telemetering crew turned off their instruments. The whining eighteen-inch reel that was flinging tape across a row of fifteen magnetic heads, recording the picture the spy-bird took, slowed and droned and stopped. Out of instinct and habit Kramer pulled out his rough diary and jotted down *Brig. Spiegelhauer – Permits bad wea. sta. situation?* But it was little enough to have learned on a flight to Kiska, and everything else seemed going well.

Captain Mabry fetched over two mugs of hot cocoa. 'Sorry,' he said. 'Cain't be helped, I guess.'

Kramer put his notebook away and accepted the cocoa.

'Beats U-2in',' Mabry went on. 'Course, you don't get to see as much of the country.'

Kramer could not help a small, involuntary tremor. For just a moment there, looking out of the spy-bird's eyes, he had imagined himself actually in the air above yute territory and conceived the possibility of being shot down, parachuting, internment, the Blank Tanks, 'Yankee! Why not be good fellow? You *proud* you murderer?'

'No,' Kramer said, 'you don't get to see as much of the country.' But he had already seen all the yute country he ever wanted.

Kramer got back in the elevator and descended rapidly, his mind full. Perhaps a psychopath, a hungry cat or a child would have noticed that the ride downward lasted a second or two less than the ride up. Kramer did not. If the sound echoing from the tunnel he walked out into was a bit more clangorous than the one he had entered from, he didn't notice that either.

Kramer's mind was occupied with the thought that, all in all, he was pleased to find that he had approached this close to yute territory, and to yute Blank Tanks, without feeling *particularly* afraid. Even though he recognized that there was nothing to be afraid of, since of course the yutes could not get hold of him here.

Then he observed that the door Mabry opened for him led to a chamber he knew he had never seen before.

They were standing on an approach stage and below them forty-foot rockets extended downward into their pit. A gantry-bridge hung across space from the stage to the nearest rocket, which lay open, showing a clumsily padded compartment where there should have been a warhead or an instrument capsule.

Kramer turned around and was not surprised to find that Mabry was pointing a gun at him. He had almost expected it. He started to speak. But there was someone else in the shadowed chamber, and the first he knew of *that* was when the sap struck him just behind the ear.

It was all coming true: 'Yankee! Why not be honest man? You *like* murder babies?' Kramer only shook his head. He knew it did no good to answer. Three years before he had answered. He knew it also did no good to keep quiet; because he had done that too. What he knew most of all was that nothing was going to do him any good because the yutes had him now, and who would have thought Mabry would have been the one to do him in?

They did not beat him at this point, but then they did not need to. The nose capsule Mabry had thrust him into had never been designed for carrying passengers. With ingenuity Kramer could only guess at, Mabry had contrived to fit it with parachutes and watertight seals and flares so the yute gunboat could find it in the water and pull out their captive alive. But he had taken 15 and 20-G accelerations, however briefly. He seemed to have no serious broken bones, but he was bruised all

over. Secretly he found that almost amusing. In the preliminary softening up the yutes did not expect their captives to
be in physical pain. By being in pain he was in some measure
upsetting their schedule. It was not much of a victory but it
was all he had.

Phase Two was direct questioning: What was Ripsaw exactly? How many divisions? Where located? Why had Lieutenant General Grote spent so much time with Lieutenant
General Clough? When Mary Elizabeth Grote, before her
death, entertained the Vietnamese UNESCO delegate's aunt
in Sag Harbor, had she know her husband had just been passed
over for promotion to brigadier. And was resentment over
that the reason she had subsequently donated twenty-five
dollars to a mission hospital in Laos? What were the Bering
Straits rendezvous points for missile submarines supporting
Ripsaw? Was the transfer of Lieutenant Colonel Carolyn S.
Bucknell from Message Center Battalion C.O. to Mess Officer
a cover for some CIC complexity? What air support was
planned for D plus one? D plus two? Did Major Somebody-
or-other's secret drinking account for the curious radio intercept in clear logged at 0834 on 6 October 1895? Or was
'Omobray for my eadhay' the code designation for some
nefarious scheme to be launched against the gallant, the ever-
victorious forces of Neo-Utilitarianism?

Kramer was alternately cast into despondency by the
amount of knowledge his captors displayed and puzzled by the
psychotic irrelevance of some of the questions they asked him.
But most of all he was afraid. As the hours of Phase Two
became days, he became more and more afraid – afraid of
Phase Three – and so he was ready for Phase Three when the
yutes were ready for him.

Phase Three was physical. They beat the living be-hell out
of First Lieutenant John Kramer, and then they shouted at
him and starved him and kicked him and threw him into bath-
tubs filled half with salt water and half with shaved ice. And
then they kicked him in the belly and fed him cathartics by the

ounce and it went on for a long time; but that was not the bad thing about Phase Three. Kramer found himself crying most of the time, when he was conscious. He did not *want* to tell them everything he knew about Ripsaw – and thus have them be ready when it came, poised and prepared, and know that maybe 50,000 American lives would be down the drain because the surprise was on the wrong side. But he did not know if he could help himself. He was in constant pain. He thought he might die from the pain. Sometimes people did. But he didn't think much about the pain, or the fear of dying, or even about what would happen if – no, *when* he cracked. What he thought about was what come next. For the bad thing about Phase Three was Phase Four.

He remembered. First they would let him sleep. (He had slept very well that other time, because he hadn't known exactly what the Blank Tanks were like. He didn't think he would sleep so well this time.) Then they would wake him up and feed him quickly, and bandage his worst bruises, and bandage his ears, with cotton tampons dipped in vaseline jelly plugged into them, and bandage his eyes, with light-tight adhesive around them, and bandage his mouth, with something like a boxer's toothguard inside so he couldn't even bite his tongue, and bandage his arms and legs, so he couldn't even move them or touch them together....

And then the short superior-private, who was kicking him while he thought all this, stopped and talked briefly to a noncom. The two of them helped him to a mattress and left him. Kramer didn't want to sleep, but he couldn't help himself; he slipped off, crying weakly out of his puffed and bloody eyes, because he didn't want to sleep, he wanted to die.

Ten hours later he was back in the Blank Tanks.

Sit back and listen. What do you hear?

Perhaps you think you hear nothing. You are wrong. You discount the sound of a distant car's tires, or the crackle of metal as steam expands the pipes. Listen more carefully to these sounds; others lie under them. From the kitchen there is a grunt and hum as the electric refrigerator switches itself on. You change position; your chair creaks, the leather of your shoes slip-slides with a faint sound. Listen more carefully still and hear the tiny roughness in the main bearing of the electric clock in the next room, or the almost inaudible hum of wind in a television antenna. Listen to yourself: Your heartbeat, your pulse in your chin. The rumble of your belly and the faint grating of your teeth. The susurrous of air entering your nostrils. The rub of thumb against finger.

In the Blank Tanks a man hears nothing at all.

The pressure of the tampons in the ear does not allow stirrup to strike anvil; teeth cannot touch teeth, hands cannot clap, he cannot make a noise if he tries to, or hear it if he did.

That is deafness. The Blank Tanks are more than deafness. In them a man is blind, even to the red fog that reaches through closed eyelids. There is nothing to smell. There is nothing to taste. There is nothing to feel except the swaddling-cloths, and through time the nerve ends tire and stop registering this constant touch.

It is something like being unborn and something like never having been at all. There is nothing, absolutely nothing, and although you are not dead you are not alive either. And there you stay.

Kramer was ready for the Blank Tank and did not at once panic. He remembered the tricks he had employed before. He swallowed his own sputum and it made a gratifying popping sound in his inner ear; he hummed until his throat was raw and gasped through flaring nostrils until he became dizzy. But each sound he was able to produce lasted only a moment. He might have dropped them like snowflakes on to wool. They were absorbed and they died.

It was actually worse, he remembered tardily, to produce a sound because you could not help but listen for the echo and no echo came. So he stopped.

In three years he *must* have acquired some additional resources, he thought. Of course. He had! He settled down to construct a crossword puzzle in his head. Let 1 Across be a tropical South American bird, *hoatzin*. Let 1 Down be a medieval diatonic series of tones, *hexacord*. Let 2 Down be the Asiatic wild ass, or *onagin*, which might make the first horizontal word under 1 Across be, let's see, E - N - ... well, why not the ligature of couplets in verse writing, or *enjambment*. That would make 3 Down – He began to cry, because he could not remember 1 Across.

Something was nagging at his mind, so he stopped crying and waited for it to take form, but it would not. He thought of General Grote, by now surely aware that his aide had been taken; he thought of the consternation that must be shuddering through all the tentacles of Ripsaw. It was not actually going to be so hard, he thought pathetically, because he didn't actually have to *hold out* against the Blank Tanks, he only had to *wait*. After D day, or better, say, D plus 7, it wouldn't much matter what he told them. Then the divisions would be across. Or not across. Breakthrough or failure, it would be decided by then and he could talk.

He began to count off Ripsaw's division officers to himself, as he had so often seen the names on the morning reports. Catton of the XLIst Armored, with Colonels Bogart, Ripner and Bletterman. M'Cleargh of the Highland & Lowland, with Brigadiers Douglass and McCloud. Leventhal of the Vth Israeli, with Koehne, Meier and – he stopped, because it had occurred to him that he might be speaking aloud. He could not tell. All right. Think of something else.

But what?

There was nothing dangerous about sensory deprivation, he lied. It was only a rest. Nobody was hurting him. Looked at in the right way, it was a chance to do some *solid* thinking like you never got time for in real life – strike that. In *outside* life. For instance, what about freshing up on French irregular verbs? Start with avoir. Tu as, vous avez, nous avons. Voi avete, noi abbiamo, du habst ... Du habst? How did that get in there? Well, how about poetry?

> It is an Ancient Mariner, and he stops the next of kin.
> The guests are met, the feast is set, and sisters under the skin
> Are rag and bone and hank of hair, and beard and glittering eye
> Invite the sight of patient Night, etherized under the sky.
> I should have been a ragged claw; I should have said "I love you";
> But — here the brown eyes lower fell — I hate to go about you.
> If Ripsaw fail and yutes prevail, what price Clough's Quaker cannon
> So Grote —

Kramer stopped himself, barely in time. Were there throat mikes? Were the yutes listening in?

He churned miserably in his cotton bonds, because, as near as he could guess he had probably been in the Blank Tank for less than an hour. D day, he thought to himself, praying that it was only to himself, was still some six weeks away and a week beyond that was seven. Seven weeks, forty-nine days, eleven hundred and, um, seventy-six hours, sixty-six thousand minutes plus. He had only to wait those minutes out, what about the diary?, and then he could talk all he wanted. Talk, confess, broadcast, anything, what difference would it make then?

He paused, trying to remember. That furtive thought had struggled briefly to the surface but he had lost it again. It would not come back.

He tried to fall asleep. It should have been easy enough. His air was metered and the CO_2 content held to a level that would make him torpid; his wastes catheterized away; water and glucose valved into his veins; he was all but in utero, and unborn babies slept, didn't they? Did they? He would have to look in the diary, but it would have to wait until he could remember what thought it was that was struggling for recognition. And that was becoming harder with every second.

Sensory deprivation in small doses is one thing; it even has its therapeutic uses, like shock. In large doses it produces a disorientation of psychotic proportions, a melancholia that is all but lethal; Kramer never knew when he went loopy.

IV

He never quite knew when he went sane again, either, except that one day the fog lifted for a moment and he asked a WAC corporal, 'When did I get back to Utah?' The corporal had dealt with returning yute prisoners before. She said only 'It's Fort Hamilton, sir. Brooklyn.'

He was in a private room, which was bad, but he wore a maroon bathrobe, which was good – at least it meant he was in a hospital instead of an Army stockade. (Unless the private room meant he was in the detention ward of the hospital.)

Kramer wondered what he had done. There was no way to tell, at least not by searching his memory. Everything went into a blurry alternation of shouting relays of yutes and the silence of the Blank Tanks. He was nearly sure he had finally told the yutes everything they wanted to know. The question was, when? He would find out at the court-martial, he thought. Or he might have jotted it down, he thought crazily, in the diary.

Jotted it down in the . . .?

Diary!

That was the thought that had struggled to come through to the surface!

Kramer's screams brought the corporal back in a hurry, and then two doctors who quickly prepared knockout needles. He fought against them all the way.

'Poor old man,' said the WAC, watching him twitch and

shudder in unconsciousness. (Kramer had just turned forty.) 'Second dose of the Blank Tanks for him, wasn't it? I'm not surprised he's having nightmares.' She didn't know that his nightmares were not caused by the Blank Tanks themselves, but by his sudden realization that his last stay in the Tanks was totally unnecessary. It didn't matter what he told the yutes, or when! They had had the diary all along, for it had been on him when Mabry thrust him in the rocket; and all Ripsaw's secrets were in it!

The next time the fog lifted for Kramer it was quick, like the turning on of a light, and he had distorted memories of dreams before it. He thought he had just dreamed that General Grote had been with him. He was alone in the same room, sun streaming in a window, voices outside. He felt pretty good, he thought tentatively, and had no time to think more than that because the door opened and a ward boy looked in, very astonished to find Kramer looking back at him.

'Holy heaven,' he said. 'Wait there!'

He disappeared. Foolish, Kramer thought. Of course he would wait. Where else would he go?

And then, surprisingly, General Grote did indeed walk in.

'Hello, John,' he said mildly, and sat down beside the bed, looking at Kramer. 'I was just getting in my car when they caught me.'

He pulled out his pipe and stuffed it with tobacco, watching Kramer. Kramer could think of nothing to say. 'They said you were all right, John. Are you?'

'I – think so.' He watched the general light his pipe. 'Funny,' he said. 'I dreamed you were here a minute ago.'

'No, it's not so funny; I was. I brought you a present.'

Kramer could not imagine anything more wildly improbable in the world than that the man whose combat operation he had betrayed should bring him a box of chocolates, bunch of flowers, light novel or whatever else was appropriate. But the general glanced at the table by Kramer's bed.

There was a flat, green-leather-covered box on it. 'Open it up,' Grote invited.

Kramer took out a glittering bit of metal depending from a three-barred ribbon. The gold medallion bore a rampant eagle and lettering he could not at first read.

'It's your D.S.M.,' Grote said helpfully. 'You can pin it on if you like. I tried,' he said, 'to make it a Medal of Honor. But they wouldn't allow it, logically enough.'

'I was expecting something different,' Kramer mumbled foolishly.

Grote laughed. 'We smashed them, boy,' he said gently. 'That is, Mick did. He went straight across Polar Nine, down the Ob with one force and the Yenisei with another. General Clough's got his forward command in Chebarkul now, loving every minute of it. Why, I was in Karpinsk myself last week – they let me get that far – of course, it's a rest area. It was a brilliant, bloody, back-breaking show. Completely successful.'

Kramer interrupted in sheer horror: 'Polar *Nine*? But that was the cover – the Quaker cannon!'

General Grote looked meditatively at his former aide. 'John,' he said after a moment, 'didn't you ever wonder why the card-sorters pulled you out for my staff? A man who was sure to crack in the Blank Tanks, because he already had?'

The room was very silent for a moment.

'I'm sorry, John. Well, it worked – had to, you know; a lot of thought went into it. Novotny's been relieved. Mick's got his biggest victory, no matter what happens now; he was the man that led *the* invasion.'

The room was silent again.

Carefully Grote tapped out his pipe into a metal waste-basket. 'You're a valuable man, John. Matter of fact, we traded a major general to get you back.'

Silence.

Grote sighed and stood up. 'If it's any consolation to you, you held out four full weeks in the Tanks. Good thing we'd made sure you had the diary with you. Otherwise our Quaker cannon would have been a bust.'

He nodded good-bye and was gone. He was a good officer, was General Grote. He would use a weapon in any way he had to, to win a fight; but if the weapon was destroyed, and had feelings, he would come around to bring it a medal afterwards.

Kramer contemplated his Distinguished Service Medal for a while. Then he lay back and considered ringing for a *Sunday Times*, but fell asleep instead.

Novotny was now a sour, angry corps commander away off on the Baltic periphery because of him; a million and a half NAAARMY troops were dug in in the heart of the enemy's homeland; the greatest operation of the war was an unqualified success. But when the nurse came in that night, the Quaker cannon – the man who had discovered that the greatest service he could perform for his country was to betray it – was moaning in his sleep.